DANNY ORLIS
BUSH PILOT

DANNY ORLIS BUSH PILOT

BERNARD PALMER

ANEKO PRESS

Please note that several books in the Danny Orlis series are published by Sword of the Lord Publications and are available for purchase on their website, www.swordbooks.com.

Aneko Press *Youth*

www.anekopress.com
Aneko Press, Life Sentence Publishing, and our logos are trademarks of
Life Sentence Publishing, Inc.
203 E. Birch Street
P.O. Box 652
Abbotsford, WI 54405
JUVENILE FICTION / Religious / Christian / Action & Adventure
Paperback ISBN: 979-8-88936-000-1
eBook ISBN: 979-8-88936-001-8
10 9 8 7 6 5 4 3 2 1
Available where books are sold

CONTENTS

Ch. 1: A Summer Mission Field 1

Ch. 2: Is It Stealing? 7

Ch. 3: A Fishing Trip Without Tackle 15

Ch. 4: Doug and Hal Go to Work 25

Ch. 5: Hal Just Can't Make It 37

Ch. 6: Now for the Plane Ride 47

Ch. 7: Home Before Supper Time? 57

Ch. 8: Ed Seybold Flies into a Rage 65

Ch. 9: An Unexpected Landing 71

Ch. 10: Safer in the Cessna Cabin 81

Ch. 11: Morning Comes. A Great Decision 91

Ch. 12: An Experience Worthwhile 101

CHAPTER 1

A SUMMER MISSION FIELD

It was early morning when Danny and Kay Orlis climbed into the new little Cessna belonging to Tex Williams. Little patches of fog clung to the low places and hung suspended over the river. For a moment or two they sat in silence, waiting for the engine to warm.

Kay shivered slightly.

"Cold?" Danny glanced her way.

"Not exactly. I was just thinking how quickly things have changed for us. Last week we were so sure we would be going back to Guatemala soon. Now we're headed north to fly for Tex."

Kay brushed at her hair with a tiny hand.

"God has been working," Danny reminded her. "Even before we knew we were going to need a job He had one prepared for us in Canada."

She sighed her weariness. "I don't suppose we'll ever understand why He called us to Guatemala and then closed the door before we really had a chance to serve Him there."

Danny began to move the floatplane slowly up the river to the lake. "Probably not," he said.

"But with His help I'm not going to worry about it anymore," she assured him. "The important thing for us, or any other Christian, is to be where He wants us to be." Kay was silent until they were airborne.

"Wish we had the time to stop in and see your parents," she said when they were headed north over the Lake of the Woods.

"So do I, but Tex told the mine supervisor that we would be there before noon. We wouldn't be able to make it if we stopped."

At Kenora they touched down briefly to clear customs, get supplies and gasoline. An hour later they were headed north again.

"Danny," Kay said, peering down at the lakes and tree-studded rocks below them, "do you realize we haven't seen a road for miles and miles and miles?"

He laughed. "That's why we're up here, Kay. The mine has to have a plane to fly in their supplies and everything." He whistled a little tune. "Did you ever stop to think what a good break this is for me – for us? I'll be able to get in the flying time I've got to have and still be paid for it."

Kay Orlis breathed deeply. "I wonder if there's going to be an opportunity for us to do any Christian work at Tanbark," she murmured.

Danny glanced her way. "Have you ever been anywhere where there hasn't been a chance to work for Christ?"

He adjusted the carburetor heat mechanically and checked the map once more. Kay smiled slightly. "I'd never thought of it quite that way." Once more she turned her attention to the terrain below them. "The country's all so desolate," she said, "that I guess I was really wondering whether anyone actually lived up here – anyone except the men who work in the mines."

"We'll soon know," Danny told her. "Unless I've missed a few landmarks or misread this map we ought to be approaching Tanbark in a few minutes."

Although Danny Orlis had not been flying long, his experience in the forests of the Northwest Angle and the jungles of Guatemala helped him a great deal in finding his way. He had long since learned how to note landmarks and etch them indelibly in his mind, how to follow directions accurately, and to keep his own bearings as he did so.

While they were clearing customs at Kenora, Danny had found a veteran pilot who had flown to Tanbark many times. He learned from him the best landmarks to follow. As he came to them, he checked them off one by one, double checking himself with the map they carried in the cockpit of the plane. He had been accurate. In a few minutes the little mining village of Tanbark was visible on the horizon.

"What do you know!" he exclaimed, smiling broadly. "We hit it right on the button!"

Kay looked at him. "But isn't that what you wanted to do?"

"That's sure what I had in mind." He grinned again.

"I have more confidence in you than that, Danny," she said. "I just expect you to find where you're going."

He laughed good-naturedly. "I suppose I ought to be the same way. But to tell you the truth, I'm still a little amazed when I discover I've actually flown to the place where I wanted to go." Danny dropped the plane almost to the treetops, sought out the landing area on the lake, and nosed in for a perfect landing.

"Well, we made it," he said.

"There are some families here after all," Kay replied. "Look at the boys."

The instant the propeller stopped turning several twelve-or fourteen-year-olds ran out and stood along the shore. Their hair was long, and their faces were grimy.

"We might have known we'd have an audience if there were any boys nearby." Danny opened the cabin door and was confronted by a squat, round-faced lad.

"Hi, Mister. Where are you from – the States?"

"That's right." Danny smiled warmly. "We're from Minnesota. Why don't you help me with these tie downs?"

He moved to take the line, but half a dozen others surged about him and grasped for it.

"Here, Hal" Doug Ellis snapped authoritatively. "Let somebody take care of that who can. You can't tie a decent knot."

"I think you can manage it all right, Hal," Danny said. As he did so he got a second line, tossing it to Doug. "Why don't you go around on the other side and tie it for me?" The boys hurried to do as they were bidden.

Kay turned to her young husband. "Now why did you do that, Danny?" she asked.

"If you can get someone to help you," he told her, "you can make friends with him easier than you can if you don't."

"I think I'll try that with you," she countered. "Do you think it will work?"

"That's why I like you so much. You're always getting me to do something for you."

The boys set to work immediately and, in a few minutes, they had the plane securely tied. Danny hecked their work unobtrusively. "Thanks, fellows. Thanks a lot."

They beamed at him. "I've never ridden in an airplane, Mister," Hal said, looking up at Danny appealingly. "It sure must be a lot of fun."

Danny reached out and rumpled his long blond hair. "I'll make you a little proposition," Danny said as they walked along. "If you'll run errands for me and help me when I have some work to do, I think you might be able to talk me into giving you some rides."

Hal's blue eyes widened. "Honest?" He spoke as though he could scarcely believe it.

"Honest. Only we'd have to get permission from your parents."

At the mention of his parents, the boy paled. "You wouldn't have to talk to my dad before you'd take me for a plane ride, would you?" Hal asked. His face grew even more serious.

"Of course," Danny said.

"I guess that lets me out." Hal sighed deeply. "There's no use in talking to him. He never lets me do anything."

"If I ask him," Danny went on, "he might surprise you and change his mind."

"Not Dad," he retorted, disappointment clouding his voice.

As soon as Hal was gone Doug Ellis pushed forward. Taller than his companion, he was brusque and overbearing.

"Hey, Mister," he said, almost arrogantly, "how about letting me take that job you offered Hal?"

"We'll have to be sure Hal can't do it first," Danny replied. "Perhaps his dad isn't as opposed to his riding in a plane as Hal thinks he is."

"You just don't know old man Seybold!" Doug explained. "Why, Hal even has to sneak away just to come over here."

The boys stood around talking for several minutes. When they finally left, Kay turned to Danny, her eyes brimming.

"You know, Danny," she said softly, "I think we just saw our mission field for the summer."

CHAPTER 2

IS IT STEALING?

Hal Seybold and his friends stood along the water looking at the sleek little Cessna long after Danny and Kay had gone to the little company house where they would live for the next few months. Hal turned to his companions. "Hey, did you ever see such a cool plane?"

Pierre Duquesne went forward and touched the trim metal fuselage speculatively with a slim, brown finger.

"Do you suppose he meant it, Hal? Do you really think he'll give you a ride?"

"What difference does it make?" Doug Ellis broke in. "Hal's old man won't let him fly. That's for sure."

The chubby boy's cheeks tinged with red. "Oh, I don't know about that!" he countered. Doug snorted. "Huh!" I'll bet he won't even let you go near the air-port if he finds out about it."

Hal rose defensively. "He will too!" he cried. "I just

said that because I don't even know for sure whether I want to ride in that old airplane."

"Well, I don't think you're going to have to worry about it," Doug retorted, a sneer twisting his face. "I just talked to the pilot. He's going to give me the job. I'm going to go with him on some of his trips and help him. He said he might even teach me some things about flying."

"You're just making that up," Hal said defensively. "He didn't tell you that at all."

Doug laughed. "Wait and see! That's all I say! Just wait and see!"

When Hal got back home, his father was waiting for him. They lived in a little two-room log cabin at the edge of town. One glance at the interior was enough to reveal that it had been months since a woman had cleaned the tiny cabin. Dust was everywhere. A pile of dirty clothes lay in the far corner and there was a stack of unwashed dishes on the table.

Big Ed Seybold was standing in the middle of the room when Hal opened the door and came in. He was a giant of a man in a coarse, red shirt with a week's stubble on his face. His eyes were dark and blood shot.

"Where've you been?" His voice was a snarl.

Hal glanced up at him defensively. "Just around."

"Around where?" Big Ed insisted hotly.

The boy's voice tinged with anger. "I haven't been anywhere, I told you. I was just foolin' around with the guys."

His dad took a step toward him. "You'd better stop that back talk and get in there and get supper before I whop you!"

Hal sidled around him, keeping a wary eye on every movement that might indicate a blow was coming his way. He went to the back of the room where the stove was, heated a plate of pork and beans and got down the jar of honey.

"There's some bacon in the refrigerator," Big Ed told him, "and a couple of eggs if you want to fry them."

"I'll save 'em for breakfast," Hal said, pulling up a chair and sitting down at the table. He ate for a moment or two in silence. "Dad," he said at last, "did you see the new plane that came in this afternoon?"

Big Ed did not look up.

"It was from the States."

His dad put the magazine aside temporarily. "How did you know that?" he asked, suspiciously.

The boy's face reddened.

"Answer me!" Big Ed's voice was raised.

"I–I–I–" Hal stammered.

Big Ed got to his feet. "You've been over at the mine again, haven't you?" he demanded.

"I was only there for a couple of minutes," Hal spoke belligerently. "We saw the plane come in and the guys wanted to go over there and take a–"

His dad strode over and cuffed him savagely with the side of his hand. Hal went sprawling to the floor.

"What'd I tell you about lying to me?" he roared.

Hal rubbed the side of his face and looked up at his dad, his eyes blazing, "You didn't have any call to do that!"

"You talk back to me, Hal Seybold, and I'll give you another one! Now get up there and finish your supper!" The boy's chubby face was drawn with anger, but he did as he was told.

"I told you to stay away from that mine, and that's what I meant," his dad snarled. "We don't have anything more to do with that lousy outfit! You're supposed to stay away from them. Do you hear?"

Big Ed strode back to his chair and sat down. "We're going to get back at those bums in one way or another before we go back to the States!" he said darkly. "I don't want you having any more dealings with them, understand?"

There was a short silence. "But, Dad," the boy went on after a time, "that fellow who is flying the plane just works for the mine. That's all he's doing. He's working for them just the same as you used to do!"

Big Ed slumped even lower in his chair. For several minutes he sat there, staring at the floor.

"This Orlis guy, who's the pilot, told me he'd take me for a plane ride," Hal ventured timidly. "He said if I'd help him by running errands and things like that, he'd see that I got to take some trips with him."

There was no answer.

"I've never ridden in a plane," Hal said desperately. "Not even once. Do you think it would be all right, Dad? Just until I got to go up once and see what it's like?"

The big man shook his head. "I told you I wanted you to stay away from that mine and anybody connected with it," Big Ed snapped. "And that's what I mean. I don't want you having anything to do with them. I don't trust 'em! They did me wrong and they'll do the same to you if they get the chance."

"But Dad!" Hal protested.

"Shut up or I'll whop you again!"

With that he went back to his magazine. Hal continued to eat in silence. He was still sitting at the table when Doug Ellis came to the door and knocked.

"Hi, Hal. Done eating yet?"

"No, he's not done eating!" Big Ed exclaimed. "But if he doesn't finish pronto, I'm going to throw it out."

"Go ahead! I'm finished anyhow." Hal got to his feet and stormed across the floor.

"Where you goin'?" Big Ed demanded.

"Out with some of the guys."

"Where do you mean, 'out'?"

"Just out, that's all."

His dad put the magazine away once more.

"Now you stay away from that mine," he ordered, "and the airplanes and this Orlis or whatever his name is. Do you understand?"

"Don't get in such a sweat," Hal said, his lips curling bitterly. "We aren't going to the mine or the lake where the plane's tied down."

"Don't give me any of your lip," Big Ed snarled. "And if you know what's good for you, you'll do as I tell you."

When the boys were outside Doug turned to Hal. "See, what did I tell you?" he said triumphantly. "Your old man isn't going to let you go over to the airstrip again. That's for sure. You might as well tell Orlis so he'll give me that job. My parents don't care if I fly."

"My dad doesn't care either," Hal said. "It's just that he's mad at the mine superintendent for canning him because he kept drinking." The boy took a deep breath. "But that's not going to stop me from getting to ride in that plane. You just wait and see."

They continued to walk up the narrow, tree-lined path together. The sun had set, and darkness was beginning to close in.

"We'll see how brave you are tonight," Doug said, his voice lowering to a whisper.

Hal stopped suddenly. "What do you mean by that?" he asked guardedly.

"Just wait," Doug continued, "and you'll find out soon enough. We're supposed to meet Stan and Pierre down by the lake just before dark."

Hal Seybold's young body stiffened, and his chubby face went ashen.

"Not–not tonight!"

Doug laughed at him scornfully. "What's wrong with tonight?" he demanded. "I had to get out while I had the chance."

The other boy kicked a stone down the path ahead of him. "I just don't like it, Doug," Hal said. "I don't like it at all."

"What's the matter? Did you lose your nerve?" Doug taunted. "Are you chicken?"

"I'm no more chicken than you are. But if we get caught, what then?"

"Get caught?" Doug Ellis echoed. "Who's going to get caught? I'll lay you fifty cents to a penny that he won't even miss the fish. Besides, they just lie there and rot before he gets around to taking care of them." Hal swallowed hard.

"It isn't really stealing," Doug went on, lowering his voice to a whisper. "Everyone knows Pete just lets his fish rot in the nets. He never gets around to taking care of them."

"I still don't know whether I want to go along or not," Hal protested defensively.

Doug stared at him. "I thought you were that kind of a guy!" he snorted derisively. "I had you figured out right the first time I saw you! You're scared! That's what's wrong! You're too chicken to go on anything like this!"

CHAPTER 3

A FISHING TRIP WITHOUT TACKLE

Hal Seybold expelled his breath slowly and ran his fingers through his blond hair. Doug Ellis looked at him, smirking. "You're chicken," he lashed. "That's all that's wrong with you."

Hal bristled. "I'm no more chicken than you are."

"You've got to prove it to me!"

The melancholy hoot of an owl crescendoed and died away on the still evening air. Hal gulped hard. His fingers twisted nervously in his jacket pocket.

"I'm not the only one who isn't keen on robbing that net. Stan and Pierre don't want to do it any more than I do."

"Just wait," Doug promised, "Just you wait. They're not chicken like you are."

They walked on in silence for a few minutes.

"Where did you say they were going to meet us?" Hal asked at last.

"At the usual place."

"They're late," he said hopefully. "Maybe they aren't going to be able to come tonight."

"Now that would make you feel good, wouldn't it? That would make you feel real good."

Hal did not answer him.

While the boys waited, the last traces of daylight gave way to night. The moon was not yet up, and the darkness was deep and impenetrable.

"We might as well go," Hal said. "I don't think they're coming."

Doug Ellis put his lips together. "Listen! That's them now!"

In a moment or two Stan Baylor and Pierre Dusquesne approached them out of the darkness.

"Hi, guys," Doug said, grinning broadly.

They answered in return.

"Hal, here, has been trying to tell me that you weren't coming."

"We think we not get to come tonight, maybe," Pierre said in broken English.

"To tell you the truth," Stan added, "our parents gave us a bad time."

"You're here," Doug said, "and that's the main thing." He lowered his voice. "Are you all set?"

"All set."

They started down toward the lake hesitantly, walking single file. Hal lagged behind. Doug turned to him.

"Hurry it up, Hal! We've got a lot to do, and we haven't got all night!"

Stan Baylor hung back. "Do—do you think we ought to go through with this?" he asked.

Doug grasped him by the arm. "Don't tell me you're going soft, too!" he exclaimed roughly.

"I just don't want to get into trouble, that's all."

"You sound just like Hal." He stopped for a moment, sneering derisively. "I can see Hal being a coward, but I sure can't see you chickening out. I thought you guys weren't afraid of anything."

"Maybe it is good for to be little bit scared, huh?" Pierre managed.

Doug put his hands on his hips. His voice rose contemptuously. "All right. If you guys are going to turn soft on me, all right. I'll go it alone. But remember, if you don't go with me tonight, I'll never take you on another deal with me. You won't get another chance to get in on the easy money. Don't you forget it!"

The boys paused, looking at one another. Fear stood full in their eyes.

Doug Ellis spoke again. "I've already told you," he said persuasively, "there's nothing to be afraid of. It won't take ten minutes to slip out, find his nets, take the fish out of them, and put them back in the water. I know a guy who'll buy all we can get and pay us good prices, too. Don't chicken out on me now. If you do, it'll ruin everything."

The boys talked for several minutes. Stan was the first to yield, then Pierre.

Doug turned back to Hal once more. "How about you?" he asked. "Are you going with us or not? It doesn't make any difference to the rest of us now. We can manage easily without you."

"I–I suppose I'll go," he said reluctantly, "if the rest of you do."

"You don't have to if you don't want to," Doug Ellis told him.

Hal's temper flared. "I said I'd go, didn't I? What more do you want?"

"Now that's better." He turned to his companions. "Maybe Hal's all right after all."

Pierre and Stan nodded.

The four of them crept in silence down the path to the edge of the big lake.

Pierre glanced about nervously. "You have a boat we can use?" he asked.

"I told you I've thought of everything. Dad's aluminum boat is down here hid in a clump of brush. I put it there yesterday morning early so no one would see me."

"An aluminum boat?" Hal echoed fearfully. "We'll make an awful lot of noise in that, won't we?"

"Nobody's going to hear us! How many times do I have to tell you that?" He turned away contemptuously. "Besides, you don't have to go along if you don't want to."

"I'm going. I've already told you that."

"All right then, be quiet and do as I say. I'm running things around here."

They began to move once more toward the place where Doug had hidden his dad's little aluminum fishing boat.

* * *

Meanwhile at the cabin, not far from the place where the boys were heading, Danny and Kay Orlis were sitting at the table, their Bibles open before them in the white light of their gasoline lamp.

Danny found the place where they had been reading in their devotions but turned to Kay before starting to read.

"Well, Kay," he asked softly, "what do you think of Tanbark?"

"It's a lovely little place."

"I did some checking this afternoon," he continued. "There isn't an evangelical church in the whole area."

Kay pursed her lips. "I've been wondering about that," she said. "Do you suppose we can get some work started while we are here?"

"That's what I've been thinking about," Danny replied. "There's very little to work with. I mean there aren't any Christians here that I know of, so whatever we do we'll have to do alone."

Kay thought for a moment. "I suppose we'll have to start with personal work. I could invite some of the women in for morning coffee and try to get them interested in organizing a morning Bible study. That would be a good beginning."

"A lot of Christian women are having Bible studies like that," Danny answered. "I don't know of a better way of reaching them." He held his Bible absentmindedly. "It's going to be a little more difficult for me. I won't have a point of contact with the men. At least not very many of them."

"There are the boys," Kay reminded him. "You will have a good chance to get acquainted with them."

He nodded. "I'm going to take advantage of it, too." He paused momentarily. "But I've got to have an opening with the men. If we're going to build anything lasting here, we've got to have the men behind it, too. They've got to be reached for Christ."

The door was open, and Danny heard a faint sound outside. He straightened quickly. "What was that?"

They both listened.

"I didn't hear anything," Kay said.

Danny got up and moved to the door. "It sounded like something scraping on the sand."

Kay joined him. "You must be imagining things, Danny," she said. "I still don't hear anything."

"I'm not imagining it, Kay. I heard something; it sounded like a metal boat scraping on the beach. Did you notice whether any boats are being kept close by?"

Kay shook her head. "But I wasn't particularly looking for any," she told him.

Danny heard the sound again. "Where's the flashlight, Kay? I'm going out there and see what's going on."

She went into the other room and got the light for him. "It's probably just some fishermen. You know, Dad Orlis told us that a lot of men are fishing nights now."

"Maybe that's all it is, but I'm going out and see. It sounds to me as though someone is trying to steal a boat. They're trying to be too quiet about it."

* * *

Doug Ellis and his friends crept stealthily through the brush to the place where Doug had hidden his father's aluminum boat.

Hal Seybold glanced apprehensively about. "Is that someone coming our way?"

Doug froze, and for a moment or two stared fearfully into the darkness. "I–I don't see anything."

"Neither do I," Stan Baylor put in.

Hal grasped Pierre by the arm. "Look! Down there by the water!"

"That's only a clump of brush," Pierre whispered, his voice tense.

Doug snorted. "Hal, one more deal like that and we're sending you home. If you keep that up, you'll have us all jittery."

They found the boat and pushed it across the sand into the water. It made a dry, rasping sound that drove to the very depths of Hal's heart. Perspiration came out on his forehead and his hands began to tremble. He wanted to turn back. How he wanted to turn back! But how could he with Doug Ellis beside him and with Pierre and Stan along?

Pierre, who was standing to one side, tensed as Doug stepped noisily into the aluminum boat.

"This boat, she makes lots of noise," he said, "even now, while we are at the shore. And it will be worse when we start to row."

Doug Ellis became irritable. "I've told you a hundred times that it was the best I could do. Besides, nobody is going to hear us. Nobody is out at this time of night."

"Maybe," Stan said, "and maybe not. But I can tell you this much. If they do catch us, we're going to be in awful trouble. It–it isn't right to do what we're going to do!"

"Come on and get in if you're coming with me. If you're not coming, beat it! I'm getting fed up with you guys!"

They were just getting into the boat when Danny flicked on the flashlight and held them in its steady beam. "What's going on here?" he asked quietly.

The boys did not speak. They could not.

"What are you guys doing?" he persisted. His voice was gentle enough but there was no mistaking his firmness.

Doug was the first to find his voice. "N-n-nothing. We-w-we were just going fishing."

"Going fishing after dark?"

"Sure, why not? That's when they bite the best."

The Orlis boy moved close to the boat and shined the light in it. "Where's your fishing tackle?" he asked.

"I-I-Isn't it along?" Doug looked at his companions. "You guys must have forgotten it," he lied.

Danny surveyed them all critically.

"I think you guys had better put the boat back where you got it," he said. "It's too dangerous to be out on a lake at night."

"But it's my dad's boat," Doug protested. "I don't have to ask you or anyone else whether I can use it."

"Does your dad know you're going to use the boat tonight?"

"Sure he does."

"There's no point in going out fishing if you don't have any fishing tackle," Danny said. "I still think you'd better leave the boat here."

"We'll go out if we want to, and you're not going to stop us!"

Danny stepped closer. "Let's go and see your dad. If he knows you have his boat and doesn't care, it certainly is all right with me."

The boys stared at Danny in dismay.

CHAPTER 4

DOUG AND HAL GO TO WORK

When Danny Orlis finally got back to the little cabin on the lake, Kay was still waiting up for him. At the sound of his footsteps, she got up and unlatched the door.

"What took you so long, Danny?" she asked. "Did you see anyone out there?"

He took off his coat before answering her. "I knew I'd heard someone," he said. "It was some of the boys who greeted us this afternoon – four of them."

"Boys? What were they going to do out on the lake at this time of night?"

"That's what I asked them," he said. "They tried to tell me they were going fishing, but I'm afraid they weren't telling the truth. They didn't even have any fishing tackle along."

She was silent for a time.

"Have you got any milk in the refrigerator, Kay?"

"I think so," she replied.

She started to get up, but he stopped her quickly.

"I'll get it. I just wanted to know if we had any."

He went over to the cupboard, got a glass, and poured the milk slowly. Kay pulled a chair up to the table and sat down across from him. "What's the matter, Danny?" she asked after a time. "You act worried."

"I am concerned," he told her. "The things those boys told me didn't ring true. First, they tried to make me think they were going out fishing. When they saw I wouldn't buy that they tried to tell me they were just going out to row around for fun."

"I suppose a story like that could be true," she said, "but it does seem strange they would be going out on the lake at night just for fun – especially when they live here all the time."

"That's exactly what I think."

He shook his head thoughtfully. "No, it's more than that."

Kay saw that he was moving his hands nervously. "Do you have any real evidence, Danny?" she asked.

He sat back and crossed his legs. "No, not really, but I do know boys. And I've seen quite a few who have been doing something they shouldn't when they've gotten caught. I know I had those guys red-handed, but I wasn't able to get anything that would let me accuse them."

Kay moved closer to him and tenderly laid her hand on his. "What are we going to do about it, Danny?" she asked after a time, "Or is there anything we can do?"

He pursed his lips and shook his head slowly. "I don't know what to do yet," he said, "but we can't let them go on the way they are without trying to do something to help them – that's for sure."

His young wife glanced up at the clock and started to get to her feet. "We'd better turn in, Danny. We've got to get up awfully early in the morning."

As Danny and Kay knelt to pray before going to bed, Doug and Hal and their companions were foremost in their minds. For a long while they prayed for them.

* * *

The following morning Doug Ellis got up fully an hour before he usually did. Trying to hide his concern, he left the house before breakfast and went over to the little shack where Hal lived with his dad.

The door to the Seybold house was closed when he got there, and no smoke was coming from the chimney. Doug paused for a moment, studying the cabin intently. There was no one stirring inside. Hal and his dad, Big Ed Seybold, must still be in bed.

The Ellis boy stole quietly to the window and scratched on the screen with one finger. "Hal!" he called under his breath. "Hal! Wake up!"

The shade was up, and he could see his friend lying on the bed. He stirred sleepily as Doug called again, and for a brief instant opened his eyes.

"Hal! Are you awake?"

At last Hal Seybold sat up slowly and looked about. At first he scarcely realized that Doug was waiting for him outside. When he did, he jumped out of bed and came to the window. "Doug!" he cried. "What are you doing here? What do you want?"

His friend put a warning finger to his lips. "Don't talk so loud, Hal. I've got to see you right away. Is your dad awake?"

"Him?" Hal exclaimed scornfully. "You don't have to worry about waking him up. He's sleeping off a drunk. He wouldn't wake up unless you set off a bomb in the house. No, I won't see anything of him until noon or after."

"Get dressed and come out right away," Doug said, concern edging his young voice. "I've got to talk to you."

Hal Seybold caught his breath sharply. "There isn't anything wrong, is there?" he demanded.

"Nope," Doug retorted scornfully. "I've just got to talk to you, that's all."

In a couple of minutes Hal Seybold was dressed and outside. "What is it, Doug?" he asked. "What's the matter? Did that Orlis guy go over and squeal to your dad?"

Doug Ellis shook his head. "He hasn't been over to our place yet as far as I know. But that's what I've got to see you about. We've got to figure out some way to stop him before he does go and see Dad."

"Yeah."

Hal picked up a stone and half-heartedly threw it at a chipmunk. "But how are we going to manage that if he decides to do it? Answer me that."

"We'll talk to him first," the Ellis boy said, "and see just what he's got in mind. Then maybe we'll know what would be best."

They started to walk toward the place where Danny had landed and tied down his plane. Doug did not speak for a minute or two. "You know something, Hal," he said after a time. "I wasn't really going to steal those fish at all. I just wanted to scare you guys. I wanted to see how much nerve you'd have if we were doing something like that."

His chubby companion eyed him suspiciously. "Maybe you weren't," he said, "but you sure didn't talk that way last night. It sounded to me as though you really meant business."

"But I didn't. I was just kidding. Honest, I was."

"That's a screwy thing to be kidding about if you ask me." Hal pulled his lower lip between his teeth in a nervous gesture.

"Well, I didn't intend to steal those fish," Doug protested lamely. "And that's the truth. Use your head, Hal. Who would want to steal a little thing like fish?"

Doug took a deep breath. "You'd have to steal a whole truckload to make it worthwhile, and then you'd have to sell them quick or they'd spoil. If I were going to steal something, I'd want it to be worth some money."

Hal did not answer immediately. He looked up and saw that Danny Orlis was striding toward them, whistling a little tune.

"There's Orlis now," he whispered under his breath.

Doug Ellis stiffened and his face went white.

"Come on, Hal. Let's go over and see him." He breathed deeply. "But let me do the talking. You just stand there and agree with me."

"Okay," Hal agreed, "but be careful. He's plenty sharp. We can't get along with trying to fool him."

The boys hurried over to meet Danny.

"Hi, guys," Danny said agreeably. "How're things going?"

They both answered him, forcing smiles to their lips.

"I was just thinking about you," he continued.

Hal swallowed hard, and the color faded from his cheeks. He shifted from one foot to the other.

"You–you were?" he echoed.

"In fact," Danny went on, "I've been doing a lot of thinking about you guys since last night. What were you really doing out there?"

Doug laughed uneasily, as though it wasn't very important.

"Like I told you, Mr. Orlis," he went on, "we weren't doing anything in particular. We were just fooling around. It wasn't anything to get so upset about."

Danny leaned against a tree and grinned at them. "You know," he said, "I can't quite figure that out. It seems strange to be 'fooling around,' as you call it, so late at night. It's an easy way for a bunch of guys to get into trouble."

"What kind of guys do you think we are, anyway?" Doug protested, his voice rising indignantly. "We're not going to get into any trouble, don't worry about that."

"Most guys don't plan on getting into trouble. It usually sneaks up on them. And it often starts by staying out late at night and fooling around when they should be home."

The boys stared at him strangely. Doug took a deep breath and expelled it slowly.

"You–you aren't planning on telling my dad, are you?" he asked. "About the guys and I going out in his boat. I mean, starting to go out in his boat."

"I don't know," Danny replied. "To be truthful with you, I haven't decided yet."

"We really didn't do anything," the Ellis boy said depreciatingly. "We didn't even put the boat in the water after you came out and talked to us. We decided you'd given us good advice and that we'd better go home and go to bed."

Danny studied Doug and Hal with care.

"We don't really care whether you tell him or not," Doug went on. "We know we were doing wrong by taking the boat without permission, and we've already decided that we're not going to do it again. Of course, if you tell on us, Dad will just get mad and take away my privileges for a couple of weeks."

"I'm glad to hear you say that you know you did wrong and that you're not going to do it again."

"I wouldn't have even thought about taking the boat out last night," Doug said. "I wouldn't have considered such a thing if the other guys hadn't kept after me to do it. It wasn't Hal's fault or mine. It was those other two guys."

Hal Seybold glanced at Doug indignantly but said nothing.

"I suppose I'd better be going," Danny said after a moment or two. "I've got a lot of things to do this morning."

He started away. "So long."

Doug Ellis grasped his arm appealingly. "You aren't going to tell on us, are you, Mr. Orlis?" he pleaded. "Are you?"

Danny looked at him evenly. "It's like I said. I haven't made up my mind yet, Doug. I want to think on that for a while."

He started toward the company office, and Doug and Hal fell in beside him without saying anything.

After a moment or two, Doug spoke again. "Do you remember about the job you promised us when you got here yesterday, Mr. Orlis?" he asked. "You said that you'd give us some airplane rides if we'd help you by running errands and getting things for you?"

Danny smiled down at them. "That's right," he said. "Of course, you'll have to have written permission from your parents before we do that, saying that it's all right for you to fly with me. But if you can get that, I'll be glad to give you rides when I can. And I might even be able to give you a little cash for helping me, too."

A strange, hurt look came into Hal's face. He started to speak, but the words would not come. Doug answered quickly. "We can get our parents' consent, all right. That won't be any problem. When do you want us to start? And what do you want us to do?"

"You can start right now if you want to," Danny said. "Take this requisition slip and go over to the supply room and get a box of tools for me."

They went off together, briskly.

Doug Ellis grinned his relief. "We're really in luck today," he said. "Orlis is not only going to let us work for him, he's going to keep his mouth shut about what happened last night."

Hal pursed his lips.

"You wait and see," his companion countered. "I know what I'm talking about."

They walked on together for a hundred yards or so.

"See, when you stick to me," Doug boasted, "you don't have any troubles. I know how to take care of things."

Hal Seybold scowled, and the corners of his mouth firmed to a thin, hard line. "You can laugh," he said a moment later, "but things aren't working out so well for me."

Doug faced him. "What do you mean?"

"I don't know why I'm kidding myself," he went on. "You can get permission from your parents to fly, but there's no use in my thinking about it. My old man won't let me; he never lets me do anything."

Doug laughed. "If you do as I tell you," he answered his friend proudly, "you don't have a thing to worry about. Just trust me. I can take care of everything."

Hal stared at him in disbelief. "You don't know my old man. Nobody can change his mind once he's set on something."

"Wait until I get to work," Doug went on. "I've already got a good idea that will fix everything."

When they got back with the tools, Danny was already working hard on the plane. They stood around for several minutes, curiously. At last, he paused and looked up.

"I've been wondering about something, guys," he began. "Are there any churches here in Tanbark?"

They eyed him curiously.

"There's a little one," Doug said depreciatingly, "but nobody goes."

"Why not?"

Doug laughed. "I guess we're too tough for that."

Danny Orlis laid aside his wrench. "No one is too tough for Christ," he said simply. "The Bible says, *Whosoever comes to me I will in no wise cast out.*"

Doug Ellis shifted uneasily from one foot to the other and glanced away.

"I've known a lot of guys who thought it was only the weaklings who give their hearts to Christ," Danny continued, "but that's not true." He leaned back and told them of some of the missionaries he and Kay had known and what they were like. The boys listened intently.

"And then there was Dale Walsh, my brother's friend," he continued. "Dale kept telling himself that he wasn't going to be a weakling. Well, he got with a gang about his age in school who felt the same way. They went their own ways and wouldn't listen to anyone. It wasn't long until Dale found out where he was headed – and that was for trouble. Plenty of trouble."

"W-w-what do you mean?" Hal asked. His voice quavered uncertainly.

"His gang of high school friends," Danny went on, "began to bully the other kids and finally stole a car. Dale's friend went back to the Boy's Juvenile Center and Dale almost went, too. It was then that Dale realized he was on the wrong road and what would happen to him if he stayed there. He gave his heart to Christ. Now he wonders why he didn't do it a long time ago."

Hal Seybold squirmed. The color went out of his cheeks, and he brushed his hand through his hair nervously.

CHAPTER 5

HAL JUST CAN'T MAKE IT

The weeks that followed raced by with abandon. The mine was running three full shifts around the clock and Danny Orlis was kept busy from dawn to dark six days a week flying in supplies. It seemed to Danny that he and Kay seldom had any time to be alone together.

"Tex was certainly right when he said I'd be piling up the hours on this job," Danny said to his young wife. "I'm getting so I could fly that plane in my sleep."

Kay laughed good naturedly. "You'd better not try it," she told him.

"No fooling," Danny went on. "I've already got enough time to get my next license. I've really been piling up airtime."

He toyed with his coffee cup absent mindedly. "It's strange how much confidence a little regular flying gives a person," he said. "The way it was going back in Pawhasset, it would have taken me a year or two to have gotten in the air hours I've got already."

Kay filled his cup once more. "I've been so concerned about the boys lately, Danny," she said. "How is it going with them?"

The smile left his face. "I wish I knew," he said softly. "I sure wish I knew."

Kay leaned forward and rested her elbows on the table. "They haven't responded to the gospel, have they?"

"They don't respond at all," he said, taking a deep breath, "to anything."

He sipped his coffee a moment before continuing. "Oh, they're friendly enough when I meet them around town or down where I keep the plane, and they keep pestering me to let them fly with me somewhere. But if I try to talk with them about sin or Christ or anything like that, they clam up – but good."

Kay sighed deeply. "I know just what you mean," she said. "I've been trying to deal with their mothers, too, but I've never been able to get very far with them, either." Her face darkened with concern. "These people just aren't interested in spiritual things."

"It seems hard to us trying to work here," Danny went on, "but actually, I don't think the people here are so very much different from people anywhere else. I don't suppose there are very many people anywhere who are really interested in hearing about the Lord Jesus. That's why we've got to work and pray so hard in order to accomplish anything, wherever we serve Him."

Kay nodded her agreement.

* * *

It was a warm, lazy afternoon and Hal and Doug Ellis and their friends were swimming at an isolated spot in the lake not far from the little cabin where Kay and Danny Orlis lived. They had crawled out of the water and were sitting in the shade of a huge pine tree. The Ellis boy was leaning against the trunk, his eyes closed.

"This is great," he said. "This is really great. I only wish we never had to go back to school. Wouldn't that be something?"

Pierre Duquesne's young face darkened, and his eyes flashed their anger. "As long as we've got that same old teacher," he said hotly, "I wish we didn't have to go back there either! Everything I did she gave me a bad time."

Doug straightened and grinned down at him scornfully. "I thought you were going to get even with her," he taunted. "Or didn't you mean it?"

Pierre snorted his disgust. "Someday I will get even with her," he vowed. "You just wait and see! I'll get even with her!"

"Why wait until some day?" Doug asked, his eyes narrowing. "We'll help you right now, won't we, guys?"

Hal Seybold stirred uneasily. "That depends," he countered. "I–I don't know whether I'd want to help you or not. I've got to know what you're going to do before I'll tell you I'll help you."

Doug Ellis took his knife from his pocket and opened it absent-mindedly.

"You wouldn't be interested," he said, scorn tinge-
ing his voice. "I can tell that already. You've got to
have some backbone to do what I'm thinking of. As
far as I'm concerned, you're fresh out of backbone."

Hal eyed his companion evenly. "That night down
by the lake was close enough for me," he said. "I don't
care what you guys say or do, I–I don't want to do
anything that's going to get me into any trouble."

"There you go again!" Doug exploded derisively.

"What a foul ball you are! Always making things
difficult. Just for that, we're not going to take you with
us – even if you beg us. You're going to miss all the
fun. We're not going to let you go along!"

Hal moved closer and looked from one to the
other. "What are you going to do, Doug?" he asked,
forcing out the words. Doug Ellis snorted in disdain.
"None of your business." He poked Hal in the chest
with his finger, imperiously. "You said you didn't
want to go along with us, so we're going to let you
stay at home. You're too chicken to go along anyway."

"M-maybe I–I'd change my mind," Hal Seybold told
him, "if I knew for sure what you're planning to do."

Doug turned to Pierre and Stan, shaking his head
for emphasis. "It's too late now," he said. "We've
already made up our minds. You're out, Hal. Even
if you get down on your knees and beg us, we're not
going to take you along, are we, guys?"

The other boys shook their heads solemnly.

"Where–where are we going?" Stan asked. He spoke uncertainly.

Doug lowered his voice to a harsh, expectant whisper. "I can't tell you now," he said tautly, with a significant glance in Hal's direction. "Nobody's going to get a chance to louse this up! Nobody!"

"You can trust me," Hal said calmly. "Even if I don't go along with you I–I'll not squeal on you."

"We're not going to give you the chance." Doug moved closer to Stan and Pierre. "As soon as we're alone I'll tell you all about it."

He started to laugh to himself. "You can bet we're going to get back at that teacher who's been giving you so much trouble, Pierre. But good! And she won't even know what hit her!"

Hal Seybold felt a little ball of ice in his stomach. He was a coward, he told himself. The guys would all know he was too scared to go with them. They would never have anything more to do with him!

He walked over to the place where he had laid his clothes. The other fellows had changed from their swimming trunks and were almost dressed. They looked his way but did not speak to him.

Stan lowered his voice until Hal scarcely heard him. "What are we going to do, Doug?" he asked. "Have you got it planned out?"

"Keep your shirt on," the ringleader said. "When the time comes, I'll tell you what we're going to do. That will be plenty soon enough."

Hal Seybold dressed alone, and leaving his companions, he walked back alone to the little shack where he lived with his dad. Doug and the others went off in the opposite direction, their eyes bright with excitement and with scorn for him for being too afraid to go with them.

When he got back to the little two-room cabin, his dad, Big Ed Seybold, was lying on the bed in one corner. The boy entered quietly. Big Ed rolled over and sat up, staring almost belligerently at Hal. "Now where've you been, young man?" he demanded.

The boy did not answer him.

Big Ed's voice rose. "I say, where've you been?" He swore. "Answer me or I'll bash you one!"

Hal's lower lip curled defiantly. "What's it to you where I've been?" he snapped.

"You're my kid!" Big Ed growled. "That's why it's something to me where you've been!"

He lurched to his feet. "If you start givin' me that lip again, so help me I'll thrash you the way you deserve. That's the trouble with you, Hal Seybold! You're just like your mother!"

He cursed again, savagely. "She didn't amount to nothin' when I married her and she's worse now! And you're gettin' more like her every day!"

Big Ed swore again. "You sass me once more, young man, and I'll make you wish you hadn't!" He stumbled unsteadily. "You're still my kid and you've got to do what I tell you! Just remember that! Give me more of your lip and I'll whale you until you can't sit down for a week!"

Hal Seybold sidled toward the door. The icy lump of pain continued to grow with each passing minute. He should have gone with Doug and Stan and Pierre – that's what he should have done. But how could he? How could he go and do something that was against the law when Danny Orlis was preaching to him all the time? When Danny was telling him how wicked he was?

Hal sighed miserably and made his way out to a big tree a safe distance from the house. He sat down wearily for a moment or two on the opposite side where his dad wouldn't be able to see him.

Being a Christian sounded great all right. Danny Orlis made it sound as though it was the most important thing in all the world. But it wasn't for him – that much was certain.

He got to his feet and kicked angrily at a pinecone, sending it bouncing down the narrow trail. He should have gone with the guys! That's what he should have done! Now he was an outcast! The guys never would have anything more to do with him.

* * *

Hal saw Doug Ellis the following morning, but his friend was very mysterious about what he and the others had done the night before. Hal asked him, curiously, as soon as they met.

"What did you do last night?" Hal began as soon as they were alone.

Doug grinned. "That would be telling."

"Did you get even with her?" the Seybold boy persisted.

"What'd I tell you we were going to do?" Doug asked. "Didn't I say we were going to get even with her?"

Hal lowered his voice and leaned forward tensely. "What did you do?" he asked. "Come on – tell me."

Doug snorted derisively. "You know better than to ask that. If you want to find out what we're doing, you'll have to go along the next time without all that whining about getting into trouble."

Hal started to answer him, but Danny Orlis came up just then and he stopped short.

"Hi, Danny," the boys said.

"Hi." He squatted down beside them. "Did you guys hear the news?"

He looked from one to the other, a question in his eyes.

"What news?" Hal asked. "We haven't heard anything."

Danny put his lips together. "I thought maybe you might have heard about it. I was just talking to the constable. He said somebody broke into the schoolhouse last night and did a lot of damage."

Hal Seybold sucked in his breath sharply. "No foolin'?"

"That's right," Danny Orlis replied. "He said they must have done four or five thousand dollars' worth of damage. Ruined seats, broken blackboards and everything."

Doug Ellis cringed, and his cheeks paled slightly. Hal was the one who spoke.

"What is the constable going to do about it?" he wanted to know.

"First of all," Danny said, eyeing the boys significantly, "they're going to find out who did it so they can make them pay for all the damage they did. After that, I don't know. They might put them in jail."

Doug forced an odd little laugh. "They–they'll probably never find out who did it," he said lamely. "They never do."

"Oh, they'll find out," Danny assured them. "Sooner or later they'll find out who did it. To tell you the truth, they've got some good clues already."

There was a short, uneasy silence.

"I–I sure hope they catch them," Doug Ellis said with forced bravado. "Guys hadn't ought to get away with–with things like that."

He took a deep breath and changed the subject. "By the way, Danny," he continued, "when are you going to give us that plane ride?"

"When do you want to go?" he asked.

"Right now."

"Can't take you with me today," he said. "I've got too big a load. But I'll tell you what I'll do. If you get a signed statement from your parents that they know you're going with me and it's all right, I'll take you with me tomorrow." He paused momentarily. "That is, if I have room."

Hal Seybold felt the color drain from his cheeks.

What good had it done for him to do all that work for Danny? His dad would never give his permission to go along.

CHAPTER 6

NOW FOR THE PLANE RIDE

Doug Ellis and Hal Seybold talked with Danny for a long time before leaving him and walking off toward the village together. As soon as they were out of hearing distance Hal turned to his companion. "What did you guys do, wreck that school house?" he demanded harshly.

Doug's eyes narrowed. "Whatever gave you that crazy idea?" he asked scornfully. "What are you trying to blame on us now?"

"Well," Hal said, "you and Pierre bragged that you were going to get even with the teacher for what she did to him last year." He lowered his voice to a whisper. "Is that where you were last night, Doug? Were you the guys who tore up the school?"

Doug Ellis looked about quickly as though to be sure no one had heard his friend. Then he turned and faced Hal, towering a head above him. For a full minute he glared down at him, his temper boiling and his eyes flashing. "Don't you tell anyone what you told me just now, Hal Seybold! If you do, it'll be too bad for you, understand?"

In that instant all the desire to have been with Doug and his friends in whatever they did the night before melted away, and he was really thankful that he had had sense enough to stay at home.

"Were you the ones who broke into the school?" he asked again.

"Now listen!" Doug exploded. "I've stood for all of that I'm going to!"

He took a step closer to his companion. "If I hear you've told anyone else we were in the school house last night or any other night, we'll all get you! And you'll be sorry! For your information we didn't go near that school house last night. We were just giving you a bad time because you're so chicken, that's all. We were at home and in bed when the schoolhouse was wrecked, and we can prove it!"

But he was unconvincing to Hal.

"Well," Hal said. "I was just asking. You don't need to get so worked up about it."

They walked on in silence. It was a full minute before Doug spoke again. "It's about time Orlis was taking us on that plane ride," he continued, changing the subject abruptly. "I was beginning to think he never did intend to. I figured maybe he was just kidding us to get us to do his dirty work for him. It'd be just about like him."

"Oh, he wouldn't do that," Hal said quickly. "He's not that sort of a guy! When he tells you something you can depend on it. It's the truth."

Doug Ellis laughed shortly. "Don't let that religion talk of his throw you," he said scornfully. "He's no different than anyone else. He's looking out for Danny Orlis and don't you forget it. All that religion he spouts is just a joke."

Hal Seybold did not answer. Somehow he knew what Doug said about Danny wasn't true, but there was no use in arguing with him. He had already made up his mind about Danny and nothing was going to change it.

After a time, Doug Ellis continued. "I'm sure glad he's going to give us that plane ride anyway," he said. "That's one thing I haven't done. I've never ridden in a plane before."

"Neither have I," Hal replied wistfully. "And from the way things look I never will. I might as well forget it."

"Why?" Doug asked. "Orlis told you he'd give you a ride, didn't he? Do you think he's going to back out?"

"No," Hal said. "He'll take me all right – if I get that paper signed. But my old man would never sign a paper that would let me go for a plane ride. He never lets me do anything. You know that as well as I do. There's no use even trying."

Doug paused and looked down at Hal, disdain growing in his eyes. "I can fix it up so you can go," he said, his voice guarded. "That is, if I want to."

"You wouldn't be able to get anywhere with Dad," Hal Seybold retorted. "He'll treat you the same way he does me whenever I ask him something. Then for a couple of weeks he'll be that much rougher on me."

He shook his head. "Nope, it's no use."

Doug snorted. "Who said anything about talking to your old man?" he asked. "That wouldn't do any good."

"But you said you'd help me," Hal countered. "You said you could get him to sign a paper for me, didn't you?"

"I said I could fix things for you so you could go for that plane ride with Orlis and me," the Ellis boy told him. "And that's what I meant."

He lowered his voice. "I can fix things so you can go on that plane ride with us. All you've got to do is have backbone enough to do as I tell you."

"Do you really mean it?" Hal asked incredulously. "Can you fix things?"

"Sure, I can fix it," Doug Ellis said. "Of course, you can't be as chicken as you were last night. You've got to have nerve enough to do your part."

"You can count on me." Hal's determination firmed. "How do you figure on doing it?"

"I've got a pal or two who'll help me," Doug went on cautiously. "I'll go to this one guy and tell him what a fix you're in. He doesn't like your old man much anyway. He'll write out a note saying you can fly and sign your dad's name to it. You can give that to Orlis. He'll never know the difference."

Hal Seybold's eyes brightened.

"Do–do you really think it'll work?" he asked.

"Of course it'll work. Why wouldn't it?"

He stopped and bent down to Hal, his voice a taut whisper. "But whatever you do," Doug warned, "don't breathe a word of it to anyone. Not even Pierre and Stan. If you do tell anyone at all, it'll get us both into a peck of trouble."

"Don't you worry about me saying anything," Hal said. "The old man would skin me alive if he ever found out."

* * *

That evening Danny and Kay Orlis stood together in the living room of their little cabin looking out over the peaceful, mirror-like lake.

"Well, Kay," Danny began after a time, "did I tell you I made arrangements to take the boys with me in the morning?"

Kay was hesitant. "Do you really think you should?" she asked him uneasily.

He half turned to look at her, frowning deeply. "Why do you say that?"

"I don't know," Kay replied. "It's probably silly, but I feel a little uneasy about it. That's all."

Danny tenderly took her by the shoulders. "What's the matter, Kay?" he said. "Don't you have any confidence in my flying ability anymore?"

"You know it's not that," she said, shrugging her shoulders. "Don't pay any attention to me, Danny. I'll be all right in the morning."

Danny went over and sat down. "You'll have to get over that sort of thing, Kay," he told her. "I'm going out a lot and we'll be hauling more and more passengers. There isn't anything to be so upset about. Besides, the boys are really excited about flying. This may be the means of reaching those guys."

Danny's voice grew even more serious as he continued to speak. "I'm worried about those boys, Kay. They're headed for trouble. Serious trouble, unless we can reach them for Christ, and soon."

Kay sat beside him and laid her hand on his arm. "I couldn't help thinking about them when I heard about the vandalism that took place at the schoolhouse last night. Do you suppose they had anything to do with that?"

Danny breathed deeply. He was a long while answering – a very long time. "I sure hate to say," he replied. "I don't have any evidence to make me think they were responsible. But there's something about those guys that really disturbs me. Something aside from the fact that I caught them taking the Ellis boat the other night and that they don't know the Lord."

He picked up a magazine and looked at it for a moment, disinterestedly. "I'm not sure just what it is that bothers me, Kay."

Neither of them spoke for a moment or two.

"I–I feel the same way," she answered.

There was a short silence.

"And there's something else that bothers me about this whole thing, Kay."

"What's that?" she asked.

"If what we hear around the mine is true, we're going to have to work fast if we're going to be able to help these boys spiritually."

"You mean that rumor about being moved?"

"I'm afraid it's something more than a rumor," he went on. "According to everything I've been hearing, they've made a big gold strike in northern Ontario. Work is going to start there in a few weeks and quite a few people from here will be transferred to the new location."

"Do you think it will affect us?" she wanted to know.

He nodded. "Unless I'm mistaken, we'll probably be among the first to go," Danny said. "This new location is quite a distance off the road just as we are here. That means they'll have to have all the supplies, machinery, and so on flown in. One of the supervisors told me only this morning that he's sure he'll be transferred."

Kay smiled wistfully. "I'm sure it's selfishness, Danny," she said, "but I'm happy about it. We'll be close enough to the Angle to get to see your parents once in a while."

Danny grinned. "I've already thought of that," he replied. "It's going to be great to be near home. But it also means that whatever we do for the Lord up here is going to have to be done right away."

The next morning Danny Orlis was supervising as two mechanics were helping to check the floats on his plane. Doug and Hal came over and stood beside him watching intently.

"Hi, guys," Danny said as he saw them. "Are you all set?"

"All set," Doug Ellis answered before his companion had a chance to speak.

"We–we've both got our notes," Hal put in. "Right here."

Danny took the notes and read them carefully.

"That's fine," he said. "I was sure your parents wouldn't have any objections, but I wouldn't want to take you unless I knew it was all right with them."

Hal shifted nervously from one foot to the other and stared at the ground, but he said nothing.

At last the mechanics finished checking the floats, and Danny examined their work carefully.

"It looks as though everything is in order," he murmured. "Why don't you guys wait here? As soon as I find out what we've got to haul north, I'll be ready to go."

With that he strode away purposefully.

Doug Ellis turned to his companion. "See!" he gloated, "you didn't have anything to worry about. He doesn't suspect a thing. It was a breeze!"

"It was a breeze all right," Hal conceded, his voice betraying his uneasiness, "if the old man doesn't find out about it. If he does, I'll really be in a fix! And so will you!"

"Keep your mouth shut," Doug warned, "and he won't find out a thing."

In a few minutes Danny was back. The smile was gone from his face.

"I'm afraid I've got a little bad news for you," he said.

Disappointment flickered in Hal's face. "You–you mean we won't be able to go along after all?" he asked.

"I'll only be able to take one of you," Danny told them. "We've got some heavy machinery to fly and there won't be room."

Doug Ellis spoke up first, boldly. "If you can only take one of us," he said, "I'll go."

Danny shook his head. "You can go the next time, Doug," he answered. Hal's the one I made the deal with first. I'm going to take him this trip."

Doug Ellis's eyes flashed angrily. "But–but–"

He was still sputtering as they climbed into the plane.

CHAPTER 7

HOME BEFORE SUPPER TIME?

Danny checked the plane carefully and noted that both gas tanks were filled.

"Are we ready to get in yet?" Hal asked him impatiently.

The pilot smiled. "As soon as we get our load," he replied patiently. "You said this was to be your first ride in a plane, didn't you, Hal?"

The younger boy nodded. "I've never had a chance to go up before," he said. "The fact is, I never thought I'd even get the chance to fly – ever – in my whole life."

"I'm sure you'll like it," Danny told him. "Most guys do."

The workmen were bringing a large box of machinery parts out to the plane.

"Is–is that what we're going to take with us?" Hal asked.

"That's right," Danny said. The mine would have

to shut down by noon if we didn't get the stuff delivered by that time."

"Isn't it awfully heavy?" Hal stared at it doubtfully. "Are you sure we can take off with a load like that?"

"Oh, yes," Danny told him. "We've weighed everything except you, and I think I know about what you weigh. We have plenty of margin of safety as far as weight goes. We don't fly unless we do."

Danny and Hal helped load the parts in the plane and the young pilot lashed them down himself.

"Well, Hal," he said when he had finished, "I guess we're ready to go."

They got into the plane and Danny showed Hal how to fasten his seat belt. There was a certain tenseness about his face. He pursed his lips and took a deep breath. "This is something," he murmured. "This is really something."

Danny Orlis started the engine and let it run at idling speed for a few minutes. While they were waiting, he glanced casually at his young companion.

Hal was nervous. Danny could see that by the way his hands worked and the way perspiration sprinkled his forehead.

"All set, Hal?" he asked when the engine was warmed and ready to go.

"I–I guess so," the boy replied, "As ready as I'll ever be."

"We'll be taking off in a minute or two," Danny said. "The way the wind is, we'll have to taxi out into the lake and turn back so we can take off against it."

Hal's mouth tightened.

"Sure wish we'd have had enough room to take Doug Ellis along on this trip," Danny began changing the subject. "He was really disappointed when he couldn't go with us."

A crooked grin lighted Hal's face momentarily. "He'll get over it," he replied. "At least that's what he would have told me if I'd have been the one who had to stay at home."

"We'll give him a ride just as soon as we can," Danny said. "It shouldn't be more than a couple of days until I have a load light enough to take him with me according to the number of trips I've been making the past few days."

He looked up at the gas gauges over either door and moved the light plane away from the dock. Carefully he headed upstream toward the big lake.

They taxied out into the lake with the wind until they had water enough behind them to get them into the air. Then Danny turned, flaps down.

"W-w-what do you do now, Danny?" Hal sputtered, trying to hide his uneasiness.

"You watch and see."

He opened the throttle, and the plane went racing forward, roaring smoothly along the water.

The wind was blowing at five or ten miles an hour, just enough to roughen the surface of the lake and make it easy for Danny to break the plane free from the water and up on the step. In that position for a brief space of time, he eased back on the controls and the Cessna lifted gracefully into the air. The plane nosed above the trees with several hundred yards to spare.

Hal Seybold stiffened and his hands clinched the arm rest convulsively. He exhaled slowly.

Once they had gained a safe measure of altitude Danny eased up on the throttle and banked gently to circle the little village of Tanbark. He looked at his youthful passenger again.

"What do you think of this?" he asked. "Still like to fly?"

Hal Seybold relaxed a little. He moved out to the edge of his seat, as far as his seat belt would permit, and stared at the scene below.

"This is really something!" he exclaimed. "Just wait until I tell the guys!"

Danny grinned at him.

"Like it?" he asked again.

"Like it?" Hal echoed. "I'll say I like it! It–it's the greatest!"

"I've been doing a lot of flying, especially in the last year or two," Danny said, raising his voice against the noise of the motor, "but to tell you the truth, Hal, I always feel the same way. There's nothing quite like it."

There was a slight overcast, but the ceiling was virtually unlimited. Danny climbed the Cessna to a thousand feet, studied his map, and headed north by north, northeast. Hal's attention was captured by the forest and the lakes that stretched endlessly below them, from horizon to horizon and beyond. It was a long while before he spoke again. At last he turned to the pilot.

"How can you tell where you're going, Danny?" he asked curiously.

"It's not as hard as it looks," Danny explained. "When you learn to fly you have to learn a certain amount of navigation at the same time. You've got to know how to read maps and how to fly by instruments. And of course you have to learn to use landmarks and that sort of thing to fly by dead reckoning."

Hal Seybold was silent for a moment or two. "Do–do you suppose you could teach me to fly?" He wanted to know. "Could you?"

"Maybe," Danny said, "if you still want to learn to fly when you get a little older."

They touched down at the little north woods mining village. While workmen unloaded the machinery, Danny checked to see there was nothing to be sent out. Hal tagged along beside him as he headed back to the plane.

"What do we do now?" the boy asked. "Do we have anywhere else to go?"

Danny glanced up at the clouds that were beginning to move in. He frowned his concern.

"You–you don't think there's going to be a storm, do you, Danny?" Hal asked, his nervousness etched in his voice. "You don't think it'll be bad enough to keep us from getting back today, do you?"

Danny looked at him curiously. There was a strange note in the boy's voice – something Danny couldn't quite understand.

"It shouldn't be too bad, Hal," he said, "but before we leave here, I want to make sure everything's all right."

He checked with the nearest weather station. Hal stood on the float, listening intently.

"There's a front moving in," Danny said moments later. "But it won't be here until the middle of the night. We've got plenty of time to get back to Tanbark."

"Then the weather's all right to fly?"

Danny nodded. "There's plenty of visibility and no rain in the area. There's nothing to keep us from going back home."

Relief flooded Hal's face. He grinned broadly. "I'm sure glad of that," he said. "I don't know what Dad would say if I didn't get home before supper time."

"Oh, we'll send word back to Kay," Danny told him, "and have her go over and tell your dad if something should happen and we were delayed. We wouldn't want him to worry."

Hal looked at Danny strangely, with something akin to fear in his eyes, but did not speak.

They got back in the plane, took off, and headed back toward Tanbark.

Hal was watching the clouds. "How long do you suppose it will take us to get there, Danny?" he asked.

"Not more than an hour." The pilot looked down at his watch and then at the map. "We ought to be home by–"

The motor coughed suddenly.

Hal stiffened. "What was that?" he demanded.

Danny caught his breath and reached over to change the throttle.

The motor coughed again.

"Danny!" Hal cried in dismay.

CHAPTER 8

ED SEYBOLD FLIES INTO A RAGE

Back in Tanbark the hours passed slowly. The clouds had been high and unbroken all day, but since afternoon they had begun to press down against the treetops. The wind whipped savage little whitecaps against the rock lined lakeshore, and every now and then a sudden flurry of rain went skittering across the water. And, although it was still August, the wind was raw and biting.

In his little shack on the outskirts of Tanbark, Big Ed Seybold waited impatiently for Hal to return home. The effects of his drinking bout the night before had long since worn off, and he was feeling miserable and ill-tempered.

"That kid!" he muttered darkly to himself. "Just wait until I get my hands on him! Thinks he can run off and do as he pleases any time he feels like it! I'll show him! He'll know he's had a hiding when I get through with him this time!"

Big Ed kicked a chair out of his way and stumbled into his bedroom. He picked up the alarm clock that was sitting on an orange crate beside his bed and stared at it, cursing savagely.

"That settles it!" he said aloud. "I ain't waitin' around here any longer. I'm going after him!"

He jerked his heavy mackinaw from a nail, put it on, and went angrily outside. The chill wind slapped him in the face and he stopped momentarily, shivering under its impact. Then he headed up the path toward the Ellis home, his feet eating up the distance in great, anger-paced strides.

Doug Ellis was sitting alone on the front steps when he approached. Big Ed stopped and turned to face him.

"Where's Hal?" he demanded.

Doug glanced up, a sneer on his youthful face. "How would I know?" he asked insolently, "I'm not his nursemaid."

"You were with him this morning," Ed retorted, his eyes narrowing. "Don't try to lie to me about that or I'll slap that silly grin off your face."

Doug Ellis paled slightly. "I–I was with him this morning," he admitted reluctantly.

"That's better." Big Ed moved closer. "He's not at home and you are. Where is he?"

"I told you I don't know." The boy's voice raised.

"It was a long time ago when I saw him. I don't know where he is now."

Big Ed grimaced and his fist drew back. "Now don't start givin' me that stuff or you'll be in real trouble. Now where is he? Where'd he go?"

Big Ed continued to inch toward Doug, his very manner menacing. The boy cringed. "I–I haven't seen him, Mr. Seybold," the boy retorted quickly. "Honest, I haven't. I haven't seen Hal since early this morning."

Big Ed's mouth drew down to a thin, hard line. "I'm not going to ask you again." The anger in his voice was all but uncontrollable. "Where did he go?"

He stood in silence for an instant, towering over Doug Ellis.

"If you know what's good for you, you'll tell me where you saw him," he rasped. "Now speak out before I lose my temper and give you the hiding you deserve!"

Doug caught his breath sharply and the color drained from his cheeks. "The–the last time I saw Hal, he was down by the creek."

Suspicion flickered in Big Ed's eyes. "Down by the creek, you say? He wasn't over there where that Orlis feller was loading his airplane, was he?"

Doug looked up at him, his gaze wavering uncertainly. "I–I guess so."

There was a short silence. Big Ed's face flushed darkly. "Where is he now?" he demanded.

The boy did not answer.

"Where is he? If you don't answer me, you'll wish you had! Where'd Hal go?"

Doug swallowed hard.

"He–he went with Danny Orlis," he blurted at last.

The silence was electric. Big Ed caught his breath. His face and neck crimsoned. For a time he could not speak.

Doug got to his feet and started to sidle away from him.

"Stay where you are!" Big Ed roared. "I'll tell you when you can go!"

The boy froze, trembling.

"Are you trying to tell me that Hal went in that plane?" he asked again. "And after I told him not to!"

"I–I don't know anything about what you told Hal he couldn't do," Doug lied, "but he–he went with Danny Orlis."

When Big Ed spoke again, his voice bellowed.

"Both Orlis and that kid of mine are going to have to answer to me for this! I'll show them they can't make a fool of Big Ed Seybold and get away with it!"

He turned on his heel and went storming away.

The instant he moved, Doug scooted into the house and shut the door.

Big Ed strode angrily across Tanbark over to the little cabin where Kay Orlis was waiting alone for Danny. He hammered imperiously on the door.

She came in answer to his knock. "Good evening, Mr. Seybold."

He glared angrily at her. "Where's that husband of yours," he snorted.

"I–I don't know," she answered. "I haven't heard a thing from them since they left this morning. Is there something wrong?"

"You can bet there's something wrong! Something plenty wrong!" Big Ed shook with anger. "And your husband is going to have to answer to me for it! Don't think he's not!"

"I–I don't have the slightest idea of what you're talking about, Mr. Seybold," Kay said evenly. "What is it that Danny has done?"

He glared at her fiercely. "You know very well what he's done. He took that kid of mine in that plane with him after I'd told Hal he positively couldn't go with him. And I'm not going to stand for it! Hal's my kid. I say what he can do and what he can't! That husband of yours had better get that straight!"

"But Danny had a statement from you that it was all right for Hal to go," Kay countered. "He told me so himself."

Big Ed snorted derisively. "I don't know what that lying husband of yours told you, but I know I didn't give Hal any statement saying he had my permission to fly with your husband or anyone else!"

She took a deep breath and expelled it slowly. "There must be some mistake," she answered. "Danny wouldn't have taken your son without a signed statement of permission from you."

Big Ed took a step toward her. "All that I can say is that I'm going to get to the bottom of this!" he stormed. "And it's going to be rough on whoever is responsible! You can tell that to that husband of yours!"

With that he turned and strode angrily away. Kay felt weak and trembling inside.

CHAPTER 9

AN UNEXPECTED LANDING

Kay remained at the door for a moment or two after Big Ed Seybold went storming up the path and out of sight. Mechanically she closed the door and leaned against it, her eyes shut. For a brief instant all was silent, save the hammering of her heart.

Then, instinctively, she began to pray. "Dear God, take care of Danny and the boy who is with him," she prayed, faltering. "Please keep them from harm and–and send them back safely."

Her voice broke and for a brief time she remained motionless, her eyes tightly closed. Kay had never before been concerned about having Danny fly, even when circumstances kept him later than usual. Yet, on this occasion, apprehension swept over her in a wave.

What should she do? What could she do – except to wait.

It was growing darker in the little cabin and the

clock on the wall ticked on monotonously as it always did, as though Danny was safely back and everything was just the same.

Numbness settled over Kay as she got into a warm jacket and went down to the mine office. The sun had set, and the little town was shrouded in the dull twilight just before it gives way to darkness. Danny and Hal couldn't be flying any more. They had to be down somewhere. Their gas supply would have long since been gone!

The supervisor at the mine office was most understanding. "I've just been talking by radio to Stan," he said. "He's the 'super' up at Wolf Creek. He didn't say anything about where Danny went or about the plane being delayed."

He turned back to the radio. "But," he continued, "I'll get him on the radio again and find out for sure."

Kay waited silently, a wordless prayer welling in her heart as he contacted the mine office at the little outpost where Danny had flown that morning.

"No," the one called Stan replied, "Orlis wasn't detained here. In fact, according to the log, he got away right on time. He should have been there three hours ago."

There was a short pause. "Anything wrong?" he asked.

The supervisor hesitated momentarily. "Hold on. I'll call you back."

He turned to Kay and spoke gently. "There's nothing to be worried about, Mrs. Orlis," he said.

"Danny's just been delayed, that's all. We'll be getting word from him before long. And as soon as we do, I'll get in touch with you."

She rested the palm of her hand against the office desk and leaned heavily on it as though a great weariness had overtaken her. "Danny should have been here a long while ago, shouldn't he?"

She spoke evenly, but with a question in her voice.

"Yes," the supervisor replied, "Danny should have been here a long while ago. But I don't really think you have anything to get unduly alarmed about. At least for a while. The chances are he had a little engine trouble and had to set down somewhere to take care of it."

He smiled reassuringly. "I hope you won't worry too much, Mrs. Orlis," he concluded.

Kay still stood there. "What are you planning to do?" she asked.

The supervisor saw that she was calm.

"I'm going to give it to you straight, Kay," he said, "because I can tell that you're not one to go to pieces. Danny is overdue. He must be in some sort of trouble. That's the only explanation for the delay. He should have been in here three hours ago."

She nodded. "I knew that."

"I'll alert the nearest airport and the Mounties," he told her. "We'll get some planes in the air just as soon as possible and comb the whole area. We'll do whatever is necessary to find him."

Kay's lower lip tightened, and her hands trembled slightly. She breathed deeply. "Is–is it all right if I sit here and wait for a few minutes?" she asked. "Until you get word from those places, I mean?"

"Of course you can," he answered, "but don't expect too much for a while. It takes time to get these things rolling."

In a moment or two he had the Mounties and the airport on the radio and informed them of what had happened.

"We'll get right on it," the radio operator at the airport replied, "but I'm afraid we're not going to be able to do anything until this weather raises. We're socked in tight. There hasn't been a thing moving since noon."

"We'll keep you informed if we get any word here."

He flicked off the radio and for a moment or two sat there, staring straight ahead.

Kay did not speak. She felt numb and cold within, as though the heart had gone out of her. She moistened her lips.

Danny and Hal were in trouble. That was all they knew!

An earnest, wordless prayer went up from the very depths of her soul.

* * *

Back in the little plane the motor sputtered again, spasmodically. Hal Seybold tightened his grip on the seat until the cords stood out on the backs of his chubby hands. His face went white.

"Danny!" he cried. "What's wrong? What's happening?"

The youthful pilot changed the fuel mixture carefully. But it was no use. The engine continued to cough and sputter. They lost speed.

Hal looked over at Danny appealingly. "W-w-w-what are we going to do?" he demanded harshly.

Danny was a moment or two in answering. "Right now," he said, smiling reassuringly, "we're going to find a good place to set this thing on the water."

"You mean we've got to make a forced landing?" he asked, his voice small and quavering as it crescendoed.

"A forced landing doesn't have to be any different than any other kind of landing," Danny went on. "Look for a stretch of water you think we can set down on."

Danny had already spotted a small lake a mile or two off to the right and was banking to make for it, but he had to have something for Hal to do. Something to keep the boy's mind occupied, if only for a minute or two.

"There's one!" Hal cried excitedly. "There's one!"

He pointed toward the lake Danny had already seen. "That's just where we're headed," the pilot announced calmly.

"Do—do you think we can make it?" he stammered.

The Orlis boy nodded grimly. "With God's help," he said, "we'll make it."

There was a prayer in his heart. "Please God! Help us to keep the motor running. Help us to make it to that lake!"

Although his heart was hammering fiercely and his forehead moist with sweat, his hand on the controls was calm as he banked the light plane about and nosed downward. The motor continued to sputter and pop spasmodically as Danny nursed it along, but it continued to run.

They were almost down to the treetops and were losing altitude rapidly. The lake they were making for was still half a mile away.

Hal was frozen in his seat. He bit his lower lip savagely and stared at the ground below.

Danny handled the limping plane delicately and with a gentle touch.

There was a continued prayer on his lips as he lowered the flaps. Now was the critical time, the moment when motor failure would be fatal.

They nosed over the trees and down toward the lake beyond. For an agonizing minute the motor sputtered and seemed to die. Then it caught again, raggedly, to bring them safely to the surface of the lake. An instant later it quit, and the floatplane dragged to a stop.

For a long minute Danny and Hal sat in silence in the little plane, looking at one another. The Orlis boy spoke first. "Praise God!" Danny exclaimed. "We made it."

Hal laughed nervously.

He reached over speculatively and touched the door handle. "I–I sure didn't think we were going to," he managed.

"God is good."

Hal stared at him. "Aren't you taking any credit for yourself, Danny?" he asked. "That was some flying! I'll bet nobody else could have done it."

"Our best isn't very much without God's help," the pilot replied. "I could never have managed without Him."

Danny reached behind him and got a long canoe paddle.

"What are you going to do now?"

"Right now," he said, "we're going to paddle this plane ashore and anchor it, so we don't smash a float on the rocks."

He got out on one of the floats and paddled powerfully. The plane was clumsy and responded poorly to the paddling, but at last it began to move toward the shore.

Sweat stood out on his forehead and back by the time he maneuvered the plane close to shore so they could pull it up out of the water and anchor it. Not until that was done did Hal speak again.

"What are we going to do now?" Hal asked. "How are we going to get out of here? That's what I want to know."

Danny turned back to the plane.

"We'll get in touch with the supervisor at the mine in Tanbark by radio," he said, "and have him get in touch with Kay and your dad so they'll know we're all right."

Hal flinched. "You–you mean he'll have to tell my dad?" he blurted.

The Orlis boy looked at him strangely. "Isn't that all right?" Danny asked pointedly.

"I–I suppose so."

"We don't want either your dad or Kay to worry about us," Danny went on. "We'll tell the supervisor what happened and about where we are so he can send someone after us."

Hal swallowed hard and ran his fingers through his heavy blond hair. "My old man's going to give me an awfully bad time."

Danny switched on the radio and began to call for the supervisor in Tanbark, scarcely noticing what Hal had said.

"KRZD calling KHAE. KRZD calling KHAE. Over."

They both listened intently, but there was no sound. Danny repeated the call letters.

"Maybe there's no one at the radio," Hal said, his concern showing in his voice.

"There's someone at the radio," Danny countered. "There always is until I check in."

He tried a fourth and then a fifth time to raise the mine at Tanbark, but without success.

"What is it, Danny?" Hal demanded. "What's the trouble?"

Fright edged his voice.

Danny shook his head. "I don't know," he said. "There's

something wrong with the radio, but I can't understand it. It was working all right when we left Tanbark."

Hal stared at Danny in desperation. "We won't be able to get in touch with them and tell them where we are!" he almost shouted. "They'll never find us, Danny! We'll never get out of here!"

CHAPTER 10

SAFER IN THE CESSNA CABIN

Hal Seybold stared wildly at Danny. "We're trapped in here, Danny!" he exclaimed. "We'll never be able to get back to Tanbark."

"It's not that bad," the pilot told him evenly. "We got down safely. That was our main problem. We could be stranded here overnight, but that's the worst that could happen now."

The boy's lips were trembling, and his chubby hands shook.

"You just don't realize what we're up against!" Hal said. We're over a hundred miles from Tanbark. And there's nothing for miles and miles in any direction but swamps and lakes. The Indians don't even come up in here very often. I tell you we're in real trouble, Danny! Nobody will find us until–until it's too late!"

Danny whistled snatches of a hymn.

"If we had our radio, it wouldn't be quite so bad,"

Hal went on. "But we don't! We can't even tell anyone where we are!"

Terror filled his eyes.

Danny put aside his tool kit momentarily and turned to the frightened boy.

"We've been forced down, Hal," he said. "There's no denying that. But it's happened to a lot of people. That doesn't mean we aren't going to get back safely."

Hal bit his lower lip savagely and fought for control.

"You don't have to be so worried," Danny continued gently. "You said that no one knows where we are. But there is Someone who knows exactly where we are. Someone who cares for us even more than Kay or your dad cares for us."

For a minute or two Hal remained silent, staring at his feet. Soon Danny continued. "The Bible tells us that God loves us so much that even the very hairs on our heads are numbered," he explained. "Since that's true we don't have anything to worry about. He's watching over us."

Hal listened almost doubtfully. "I–I'd still feel a lot better if we were back at Tanbark," he murmured.

Danny touched the New Testament in his pocket. "Have you ever considered putting your trust in the Lord Jesus, Hal?" he asked.

His companion's face colored. "I never thought much about it."

"The time is coming," Danny told him, "when each of us is going to face it whether we want to or not. Do you realize that this plane could have gone down a little while ago and killed us both?"

Hal took a deep breath and exhaled deeply.

"Would you have gone to heaven if it had?" Danny asked. "Have you considered that?"

Hal winced as though he had been slapped. "I just want to get out of here," the boy blurted. "That's all I want."

Danny did not press the subject. Instead, he picked up his tools and advanced toward the plane. There was a prayer in his heart as he set to work but not for their safety. His prayer was for his young passenger, that he might find Christ as his Savior.

Hal seemed to settle down a bit after his talk. The muscles in his face stopped twitching and he gave the appearance of relaxing a little. He came over and stood in silence beside Danny while he worked. It was a long while before either of them spoke.

"Are you finding what's wrong, Danny?" he asked.

The Orlis boy shook his head. "Not yet," he said, "but I didn't expect it would be too simple. I want to check out the ignition and gas before I do anything else. It almost has to be one or the other."

Clouds rolled over the western horizon as he went over the plane's ignition system, item by item, and the wind slapped whitecaps against the floats.

Danny glanced up. "Looks as though that weather they've been promising us is moving in," he observed thoughtfully. "I suppose we'd better get ready for it."

Hal looked up at the clouds. "It doesn't look so bad to me."

"Maybe not," Danny replied, "but don't let that fool you. We're going to have a real storm tonight. There's wind in those clouds – plenty of it!"

He put aside his tools and turned his attention to the lakeshore. "And we're not in a very good place to weather a storm," he went on, pointing across the lake. "The wind will have full sweep at us if we stay here."

Fear came back to Hal's eyes. "What can we do about it?" he demanded, his voice quavering.

Danny was silent. The lake was almost round and, as far as he could see, was without bays or inlets which would afford a measure of safety for the plane. It was too far across to risk paddling to the other side. Those northern storms were tricky. It might lie above the rim of the trees for hours, growling and showing its teeth, and creeping in so slowly there was time for every preparation. Again, the same storm could come whooping in savagely right across the sky without giving time for anyone even to seek shelter from the rain.

"There's no better place along here that I can see," Danny said at last. "We've got to stay here, so we'll just have to do an extra good job of tying her down."

He went to the cabin and got out the rope ties he always carried and set to work. Hal helped as much as he could, but Danny checked his work carefully to be sure that it was adequate.

"There are some emergency rations in the cabin, Hal," the pilot went on, "and a couple of heavy rain ponchos. Why don't you get them out, so we'll have them handy?"

* * *

Back at the mine office in Tanbark, Kay Orlis sat in silence, but her tense fingers knotted and unknotted the tissue she held. The supervisor was still at the radio trying to call Danny at frequent intervals.

"Any news yet?" Kay asked at last.

It was a useless question. She knew that, even as she spoke.

"I haven't been able to raise him yet, Mrs. Orlis," the supervisor informed her sadly. "I've two other operators trying, too. If he's listening at all, we'll get through to him sooner or later."

She fell silent once more.

"The chances are his radio is conked out," he went on. "But that doesn't matter. We'll start an all-out search in the morning as soon as the weather lifts so we can get planes in the air. We'll comb the area until we find him."

She bowed her head and prayed, her lips moving wordlessly. "O God," she began, "we just put Danny and the boy in Your hands. Take care of them. And, if it's Your will, bring them back safely to us."

Another mining official came to the door and asked if they had heard anything.

"Not a word." Concern edged the supervisor's voice.

"Have you been over to tell Big Ed yet?" the official asked.

"That's something I've got to do." The supervisor got to his feet slowly, as though it took all the strength he had just to do so. "If you'll watch this radio for a while, I'll go over and get that job taken care of. It's not going to be too pleasant."

Kay looked up. "Would I be able to help if I were to go along?" she asked.

He picked up his jacket. "Big Ed is a rough codger. I can vouch for that," the supervisor went on, "but he does think a lot of that kid of his. It might help at that for you to come along."

Kay pulled her coat about her, and they walked through the still night air to Big Ed's cabin. She noticed the lightning along the horizon and felt the unnatural, breathless hush that so often preceded a storm, but she did not mention them. The ache in her heart seemed to grow.

"I want to warn you, Mrs. Orlis," the mine supervisor said as they neared Big Ed's place. "It's apt to be pretty dirty here. He and his boy have been living here alone."

"I can imagine what it's like," she said.

He paused and glanced at his watch without actually seeing it. "You know," he went on, "Big Ed Seybold is one of the best miners we've ever had. Strong as a grizzly bear and just as fearless, and he can out-work any three ordinary men. He could still be working for us if he could just leave the bottle alone."

Kay Orlis shivered, but not from the cold. "Sin is a terrible thing, isn't it?" she asked.

The supervisor glanced at her quizzically but did not pursue the question further. "I understand it was his wife," he went on. "I wasn't here when it happened, but the fellows who were said that Big Ed scarcely drank at all until she ran away with one of the men who worked in the mine office. Left him, just like that, with Hal to raise. He started drinking soon afterward and hasn't quit since." He shrugged his shoulders. "And I don't suppose he ever will."

"The Lord Jesus is the only solution to a problem like that," Kay observed.

The supervisor knocked on the little cabin door and Big Ed responded.

"Come in!" he called out indifferently.

The mine official opened the door and he and Kay stepped inside. Ed's bleary eyes focused on them belligerently.

"Where's Hal?" he demanded hoarsely. "What's happened to my boy?"

"That's what we came to talk with you about, Ed," the supervisor said. "I've been on the radio for the past two hours, but we haven't been able to pick them up."

The big man's face whitened, and he swayed unsteadily. He put out his hand for support.

"Just as soon as the weather breaks, we'll have planes out looking for them," the mine official went on. "We should be able to find them in a little while."

Big Ed lurched into a chair and sank into it, glaring at Kay.

"If it hadn't been for that husband of yours," he muttered almost incoherently, "Hal would be right there with me tonight. He wouldn't be out in the muskeg somewhere – dead maybe." His voice broke.

"I'm terribly sorry, Mr. Seybold," Kay said. "Honestly I am. If there's anything I can do, won't you call on me?"

"If there's anything you can do!" His voice rose to a harsh bellow. "You've already done enough! I can tell you this much, Mrs. Orlis, if anything has happened to Hal, that husband of yours is going to pay for it! I'll tear him limb from limb!"

The supervisor broke in then, quickly. "Now Ed," he exclaimed firmly, "you have no call to talk to Mrs. Orlis that way. Her husband is out there, too!"

For a minute or two the miner glared at them. Then he sank back into the chair and buried his face in his hands. "Hal's all I got." His voice broke uncertainly. "He's all I got!" His big shoulders shook convulsively.

* * *

Out on the shores of a little lake somewhere north of Tanbark, Danny checked the ties that secured the little floatplane and turned back to his companion. "Did you find those rations, Hal?" he asked.

"They're right here."

"Good. I've got a little fishing tackle along, too. I've been using it to catch a few fish for Kay while I'm waiting at some of these places. In the morning you can catch us some fish for breakfast."

He asked the blessing, and they ate, watching the clouds intently, but saying little. They had washed whatever utensils they had by the time darkness settled over them.

"We'd better turn in, Hal," Danny said. "That storm isn't coming up very fast, but it'll be here before we've had very much sleep."

He got out his Bible and read a chapter from it, using the light of their little fire. Hal listened quietly, especially when Danny prayed.

"You sure sound as though you believe God is going to hear your prayers," he said almost wistfully.

Danny's eyes shone. "I know He hears," the pilot answered firmly. "His Word tells us He hears and answers our prayers."

Hal glanced quickly up at the clouds, whether to change the subject, or because of concern, Danny did not know.

"That storm is coming up faster now," the boy said. "It won't be long until it really hits."

They crawled into the cabin of the little Cessna and hunched down in the seats.

"If it weren't for that storm coming," Danny said, "I'd be a lot more comfortable outside."

"Not me!" Hal said. "There's bears out there!"

The boy curled up in the seat and went to sleep almost immediately. Danny lay there for a long time, praying for Kay and Big Ed and for the boy who was beside him. At last he, too, drifted off to sleep.

The next thing he knew Hal was shaking him.

"Danny!" he cried. "Wake up! Wake up!"

Danny stirred sleepily, then awakened with a start! The plane was lurching violently in a terrific wind!

CHAPTER 11

MORNING COMES. A GREAT DECISION

Danny scrambled upright in the seat, the last remnants of sleep torn away by the storm. The wind was snarling in from across the lake, churning the placid water to a fury and tearing at the wings of the plane.

Lightning zigzagged across the sky to light the wild, foam-laced lake briefly before cascading rain and darkness again blotted it out.

"Danny!" Hal cried in terror. "We're going to be blown away!"

The young pilot surveyed the situation quickly. He had put out extra ties and double-checked them. But there was a chance – just a chance that they would not hold.

"Where did you put those ponchos?" he demanded of his companion.

"They're in back," Hal said, grasping Danny by the arm. "What are you going to do?"

"I'm going to check the plane! I'll only be a minute!"

"You–you're not going to leave me in here alone!" His voice crescendoed frantically.

"I'll be right back!"

Danny Orlis wriggled into his poncho, pulled the hood over his head, and opened the plane door. The wind almost ripped it from his hand.

Rain slammed against his face and poured over him in torrents. He steeled himself against it and stumbled forward to check the ropes that secured the little plane. His flashlight stabbed a smooth, round hole in the darkness.

The first tie was holding, the rope strained and taut. He moved on.

The second rope was still in place and so was the third. Danny breathed a prayer of thankfulness for that.

He moved to the next, forcing himself to ignore the battering of the wind and rain, the vicious stabs of lightning, and the explosive roar of thunder. Again, he focused the pitifully weak little beam on the tie.

Danny stiffened! The rope was badly frayed. Even as he watched, it seemed to stretch a little. If that tie went, it would allow the plane a little slack, a little more space in which to surge with each blast of wind against the ties. Another would break and then another!

"O God," Danny prayed. "Help it to hold! Help it to hold!"

Hurriedly he examined the entire length of the rope. The upper end was still intact. If he could just find another anchor point closer to the plane, he–

A sudden gust of wind flung itself on the broad surface of the fuselage. The plane lurched against the ties and the frayed rope parted. Instinctively Danny realized what was happening and lunged forward, groping for the section of rope that was still secured to the plane.

The light craft was tossing wildly now with each successive wave.

Plunging into the icy water up to his knees Danny fumbled for the rope but couldn't find it! And Hal, who had been crouching tensely inside the plane, scrambled out into the storm.

"What's wrong, Danny?" Hal cried in desperation. "What happened?"

"I'm over here," Danny shouted above the roar of the storm. "Give me a hand!"

What happened next Danny was not entirely sure. The plane seemed to lift a foot or more into the air and drop violently. There was a sickening thud and the sound of tearing metal.

Hal Seybold froze. "What was that?" he asked hoarsely.

"One of the floats," Danny said, "but there's no time to worry about that now. Give me a hand with this tie!"

Somehow, they managed to get the rope, drive a stake deep into the sand, and tie the loose end securely to it.

"There," Danny exclaimed above the storm, "that's done!"

He turned toward the cabin. "Come on, Hal. Let's get inside before we get wet."

"Before we get wet?" Hal echoed between chattering teeth. "Are you kidding?"

They climbed into the plane's cabin and got out of their ponchos. Danny felt his soaked trouser legs.

"I don't know why we even bothered with those ponchos," he said, chuckling inwardly. "I think we're as wet as we could be anyway. Of course, I guess they weren't made for getting into the lake."

Hal squirmed uneasily. "What do you think about the float, Danny?" he stammered. "Do you think it's damaged very much?"

"We'll have to wait until morning and get the float up where we can take a good look at it."

Hal settled back into the seat once more, and for a time he closed his eyes. Danny did the same, but not to sleep. The wind was still lashing and tearing at the light craft savagely. With each surge against the ties a desperate, silent prayer went up.

"Help them to hold," he prayed. "Help them to hold!"

Hal, who had tried unsuccessfully to sleep, was also listening to the storm. "It's not letting up, is it?" he asked.

Danny turned and looked at him. "Not yet."

"I thought God was going to take care of us." Hal spoke accusingly, as though somehow the things that had happened were Danny's fault.

"He has taken care of us," Danny replied.

He sat up and shifted positions stiffly. It was cold in the plane.

"Are you forgetting our radio won't work?" Hal demanded. "The engine conked out, and now one of the floats is damaged. That doesn't sound to me as though God is taking care of us."

"But we're still well and we aren't hurt," Danny reminded him. "That's the important thing. You see, Hal, God doesn't promise to make everything easy for us – to answer every prayer we ask just as soon as we've prayed to Him. Or even to answer them in exactly the way we want them to be answered. He promises to give us strength and help us to take things that come. And then, in so far as it is His will, He answers our petitions."

Hal was dubious. "I sure don't get it," he retorted.

"I'm convinced that God has some purpose for these things that have happened," Danny told him. "We just don't see it yet."

"I don't think I ever will see it," Hal muttered, turning on his side and closing his eyes.

Danny managed to sleep a little after an hour or so had passed. When he finally awakened it was daylight. The rain had stopped but clouds blanketed the sky and the wind was still strong. It bent the trees and laced the lake with whitecaps.

He glanced over at his companion. "Awake, Hal?" he asked softly.

Hal Seybold grunted. "I haven't been asleep."

"You may think you haven't," Danny told him, smiling, "but you were sure sawing logs when I woke up once."

"Well, if I did, it wasn't for very long," he said. "I don't think I even closed my eyes for more than a minute or two."

He yawned and stretched. "That's the longest night I ever had in my life," he said. "I thought it would never get daylight."

"Getting hungry?" Danny asked.

"Right now I'm so cold I don't know whether I–I am or not."

The young pilot opened the cabin door and got out. "Come on, Hal," he said, "we've got lots of things to do this morning."

Hal followed him out of the plane. "Do–do you think they'll start l-l-looking for us today?" he asked, glancing at the sky.

"They'll be out as soon as they can," Danny assured him. "We can be sure of that."

He strode off into the forest and began to pull dead branches from the trees. Once that was accomplished he took his knife and made a fuzz stick of one of the driest, cutting it until it offered a hundred tiny edges for the match flame to ignite.

"Think that'll work?" Hal asked doubtfully. "Think you can build a fire that way?"

Danny reached over and rumpled his hair, grinning widely. "It always has worked," he said.

"With wet wood?"

"You wait and see!" Danny answered. "The dead branches still on the tree aren't as wet as you would think."

The young pilot built a small teepee of the driest twigs, ignited the fuzz stick, and placed it in position beneath the peak of the teepee. As the flames grew he added larger and larger sticks until in a very few minutes he had a sizeable fire crackling merrily.

Hal shook his head in wonderment. "I didn't think you could do it."

"A person can do a lot of things," Danny said, "if he knows how and sets his mind to it."

They stood by the fire, drying their clothes. As the warmth seeped through Hal, he began to smile a little. "This sure feels good," he said. "Last night I didn't know whether I'd ever get warm again."

Danny Orlis laughed. "I guess I felt about the same way."

When their clothes were dry Danny got out the fishing tackle and handed it to Hal. "Why don't you catch a few fish?" he asked. "I'm getting hungry."

The lake they were on had probably never been fished before and Hal had three fish in as many casts. They dressed them hurriedly and cooked them over the open fire.

Once they had eaten Danny turned his attention to the damaged float. Hal hunkered down beside him. "Think you can fix it, Danny?" he asked again.

"I don't know yet," the pilot replied. "We aren't going to be able to see how badly it's damaged until we get it raised up high enough to look under it."

Hal loosed the ties on that side while Danny got a long, slender pole and used it as a pry. With it he was able to raise the float.

"Now, Hal," he said crisply, "put that piece of wood under it to block it up."

Once that was accomplished Danny got down on his knees and peered under the plane.

"Is it hurt bad?" Hal wanted to know. "Is–is it anything we can fix?"

"It's bad enough," Danny told him. "I don't know what the float hit, but it's sure got a big, jagged hole in it."

Then he noticed a big deadhead, a piece of log, bobbing in the water nearby. "There it is," he exclaimed. "There's the culprit that caused all the trouble."

"If–if you ask me," he said, his voice trembling, "I don't think we'll ever get it fixed so we can get out of here."

Hal's shoulders quivered uncertainly. All the fears of the past hours came rushing back to engulf him. His eyes were wide and staring.

Danny looked at him with understanding. "There is one way you can stop being afraid, Hal," he said gently.

"Who's afraid?" There was belligerence in the bravado of Hal's voice.

"The Bible tells us," Danny continued, "that if we have put our trust in the Lord Jesus, we don't need to be afraid. We can depend on Him to guide and watch over us. We can trust Him for courage to face things that come."

Hal spoke belligerently. "I'm no more afraid than you are," he retorted hotly. "And I wish you'd quit this preaching at me. I'm getting sick of it!"

Danny was silent for a moment. "Are you, Hal?" he said pointedly. "Are you? Or are you feeling the weight of sin in your life?"

Hal's face blanched and his lower lip began to quiver. "I–I don't know what you mean," he stammered.

"The Bible says we all have sinned and come short of the glory of God."

Starting there Danny outlined the plan of salvation briefly, quoting one Bible verse after another. Hal clung to every word.

"I–I've done a lot of things I'm ashamed of," he admitted.

"We all have," the youthful pilot told him. "That's because sin rules our lives until we accept Christ. Don't you want to start living for Jesus? Don't you want to put your trust in Him?"

There was an agonizing silence.

"I–I guess I do, Danny," Hal said at last, in desperation. "I guess I do!"

CHAPTER 12

AN EXPERIENCE WORTHWHILE

For a long while after Danny Orlis and Hal Seybold finished praying, they sat beside the plane talking in hushed tones.

"This is one decision you'll never be sorry for making, Hal. Living for Jesus is the happiest way of life in the world."

Hal picked up a stone and studied it uneasily. "There's something I've done that isn't right, Danny," he said.

"Like I've told you," Danny answered, "that's all over and done with. God has forgiven you for everything you've done. It's as though it never happened."

"But this–this is something special."

Danny saw the concern in his youthful face and realized it wasn't just the weight of sin Hal was talking about.

"Would you like to tell me about it?"

Hal nodded, but it was a moment or two before he could speak. "You'll prob'ly be awfully mad at me."

He paused again. "But that note I gave you about it being all right for me to fly with you – well, my dad didn't write it at all."

Danny was startled, but he gave no sign. Hal continued, faltering. "I–I wanted to go with you on this trip so bad," Hal said, "and I knew he'd never let me – not even if he didn't care. He's so mad at the mine for firing him." He stopped, and for a moment stood there, swallowing hard. "So Doug Ellis got somebody to sign it for me."

"I'm awfully glad you told me, Hal."

Danny looked at his watch and ran his hand along the side of his face as though feeling the day-old stubble that sprouted there.

"You can see by this how sin reaches out and causes all sorts of trouble," he went on. "Your dad must think I took you with me, deliberately defying him."

"I know that," Hal answered, "but I'm going to straighten it out just as soon as we get back." There was a short silence. "I know what he'll do, though."

He shuddered. "He'll skin me alive." Danny reached out and rumpled the boy's hair. "If you'll tell your dad you're sorry and ask his forgiveness, the chances are he won't be so hard on you," he said. "Most dads want to be fair."

Hal's face darkened. "You don't know my dad."

Danny got to his feet. "We'd better get busy. We've got a lot of work to do."

He crouched once more and examined the jagged

tear in the skin of the aluminum float. "I'll have to pound this out first," Danny told his companion. "Then we'll have to find something to stop up the hole and keep it from leaking."

He set to work. "Get some pine pitch, Hal," Danny told him. "I think that will work."

The boy got to his feet obediently.

By the time he returned with the pitch on a piece of birch bark, Danny had practically finished working on the tear in the side and the bottom of the float. He stuffed rags on the inner side and, hammering the aluminum into place, he covered the tear with a thick layer of pine pitch.

"There," he exclaimed at last. "That ought to hold. At least until we get into the air and down again."

Hal smiled, but only for a moment. "That fixes the float," he said, his voice tinged with concern, "but what about the engine? We still don't have it running."

"We'll see what we can do with that right now."

Danny began where he left off the night before, working hurriedly, but with the sure, competent touch of one who knew what he was doing. The clouds that had hung so low overhead since dawn that no one would be able to fly, now gave signs of clearing. But there was another huge bank in the west. The weather was as unpredictable as it was violent. It might stay clear for only a couple of hours, long enough for him to get to Tanbark if he had the plane engine repaired so they could take off the instant the weather permitted, but not long enough for searchers to find them. And if it closed in again, it might be a week or two before planes would be able to fly.

"The ignition's working okay," Danny observed. "That means the trouble has to be in the gas line."

"We hope," Hal added.

"We hope?" Danny said, laughing. "Now what sort of talk is that? You ought to be an optimist and say, 'Sure, we're going to find the trouble first off. We'll have this airplane fixed and on the way before you know it.'"

"Do you suppose that would help?" Hal asked.

Danny chuckled. "I sort of doubt it."

He remembered as he started to remove the gas line that he had been running low in one wing and had switched to the auxiliary tank several minutes before the engine began to sputter.

"I just thought of something, Hal," he said.

He went over to the auxiliary tank and unscrewed the part that held the copper gas line to the bottom of the tank.

A mixture of dirty gas and water dribbled out.

"Would you look at this!" he whistled in amazement. "It's no wonder we were having trouble."

Hal came up beside him. "Look at all that water and dirt!" he exclaimed. "How did it get in there?"

Danny loosened the line and let the dirty gasoline run out on the ground. "I remember now," he said. "The guys drained one gas barrel when they filled that tank. It must have had water and rust in the bottom."

Danny drained the carburetor and gas lines and cleaned them thoroughly.

Hal watched the gasoline spill out of the tank onto the ground. "Have we got enough to get us back to Tanbark?" the boy wanted to know.

"Oh, yes," Danny said. "I just checked. We have plenty of gas to take us twice that far."

The youthful pilot worked as rapidly as possible on the engine. At last he had the line back in place and snugged down.

"All through?"

"We're ready to see whether I'm any good as a mechanic," he replied.

They loosed the lines, worked the floats back into deep water, and climbed into the plane. Danny touched the starter, a prayer in his heart.

The engine backfired once or twice and started. He cut the throttle to idling speed.

Hal's face broke into a broad grin. "It started!" he cried. "It started!"

"What did you expect with a mechanic like me working on it?" Danny boasted.

Hal turned his attention to the clouds once more. "How soon do you suppose it will be before we can take off for home?"

"The way those clouds are looking," the pilot said, "we'd better get out of here, and soon."

He let the engine warm up thoroughly, and then shut it off.

The clouds overhead seemed to be lifting. They were higher than before and now and then Danny saw a little sliver of blue from the sky above.

The second storm was still some distance away, but it was a big one. It lay, dark and ominous, along the west on the horizon.

Danny glanced upward once more.

The little plane might not ride out another wind on that unprotected shore.

Danny leaned forward and looked out. "Hal," he asked, "is that float we repaired leaking much?"

"Just a minute and I'll check."

He got out and examined it. "I don't think it's riding any lower in the water than it ever did," the boy said, "but maybe you'd better check it."

The young pilot stood on the good float and intently examined the one that had been damaged. It was riding a little lower in the water. That meant that it was leaking some.

Danny shoved his stubby fingers through his hair.

The plane would be sluggish to get off the lake, but if he taxied to the far end, he should be able to make it without any trouble.

"Well," he said at last, "I guess we're all set."

Hal's eyes widened. "You mean we're ready?"

"As ready as we'll ever be."

He started the engine and let it warm again. The storm was getting closer. There was no time to lose.

He taxied to the far end of the lake, thankful for

the waves that still showed whitecaps. It would be that much easier to get the plane up on the step and airborne. He remembered planes at the Angle that had to taxi out to the big lake on still days before they could break free of the suction that glued the floats to the water.

He turned the plane and cut back to idling speed.

"I think we ought to have a word of prayer," he said.

Hal nodded and bowed his head.

Danny prayed a short, simple prayer for safety.

There was a continual prayer in his heart as he opened the throttle. The Cessna was slower than usual in responding to the throttle, or so it seemed, but it began to gather speed.

Hal was looking straight ahead, eyes riveted to the shoreline that was hurtling madly at them.

Danny eased back on the controls gently. The floats fought off the waves and the plane lifted gracefully into the air.

"Thank God we made it!"

The plane skimmed over the treetops at the end of the lake.

Hal relaxed and sank back into his seat, sighing deeply. "I didn't think we'd make it."

Danny grinned and looked over his shoulder at the storm that was threatening to close in on them. He opened the throttle a little more and the plane increased its speed.

They had been in the air a little over an hour when they met another small floatplane, flying low and just above stalling speed.

"They're looking for us," Danny said. "I'll give him a signal."

He wagged the wings of the floatplane. A moment later the other fellow did the same.

"What was that for?" Hal asked.

"Just to call attention to us. He knows who we are now, and he'll radio back that we're in the air and on the way home. Kay and your dad will know that we're all right."

Hal swallowed hard. "Dad'll be back at the dock waiting for me," he said, half fearfully. "You can be sure of that."

The first person they saw as they touched down on the lake at Tanbark and taxied up the little stream to the improvised hangar was Big Ed Seybold. He was standing a step or two ahead of the others, his feet spread apart.

"See, what did I tell you?"

Danny noticed that Big Ed's face was angry and flushed with alcohol. A little spasm of fear for Hal seized him. He knew now what the boy was talking about.

Kay Orlis was standing on the bank of the creek as Danny taxied to a stop beside the dock. Ready hands reached out and grasped the wing to steady the plane and the young pilot and his passenger got out.

"Kay came running up to Danny. "Oh, Danny! Danny!" she cried tearfully. "Thank God you're home safely!"

For a long minute neither spoke. He held her close.

At last she said, "I don't think I've ever been so worried in my whole life. I thought last night would never end."

"I knew you'd be worried," he answered. "But with that radio on the blink, I couldn't let you know we were all right. Actually, we were never in any real danger. As soon as we got the float repaired and the water out of the gas line, we were able to come on in."

At that moment Big Ed Seybold laid a huge hand on Danny's shoulder and turned him about. His face was flushed, and his eyes were bloodshot.

"Orlis!" he exclaimed. "I want to talk to you!"

Danny looked up at him without wavering. "I'd like to talk to you too," he said. "I think there are some things we ought to get straightened out."

"You can bet there are some things we ought to get straightened out," Hal's dad snorted. "What was the big idea of taking my kid with you without my permission? That's what I'd like to know?"

Danny looked down at his youthful companion. The boy's shoulders twitched perceptibly, and he moistened his lips with the tip of his tongue.

"Are you going to answer me?" Big Ed demanded, "or do I have to get rough?"

"I was waiting for Hal to tell you," Danny said.

He spoke calmly in contrast to Seybold's angry voice.

"I ain't asking Hal. I'm asking you! What gives with you, Orlis? Are you trying to get out of it by laying it onto a kid? What kind of man are you, anyway?"

"I don't intend to lay the responsibility for anything I've done on anyone else," Danny told him.

"Certainly not on Hal. But you asked me a question that I feel you should have asked him."

Ed turned to his boy. "What's he talking about?" he asked.

Hal swallowed hard. "What–what he said is true, Dad. I–I was afraid you wouldn't let me go with Danny if I went to you for permission."

"You can bet I wouldn't. You can just bet on that! But that don't give him any excuse for taking you without my permission. It doesn't make any difference what you thought."

"But you don't understand. Danny thought I had permission from you," Hal explained. "He told me I had to have a note from you before he'd let me go with him. So I had one of the other g-g-guys make out a note for me and make it sound as though it came from you. That's the only reason he'd let me go with him. Honest, it was."

Big Ed stared at his boy. The scarlet flush in his cheeks gave way to a drawn, ashen look. His lower jaw sagged.

"I–I'm awful sorry, Dad. I–I'll never do it again."

At the sound of Hal's voice, Big Ed's anger seemed to kindle anew.

"You not only deceived me," he roared, "but you made a fool out of me before all these people. When I get done with you, you'll know better than to play anything the likes of this on me again."

"I feel that I should have a share of the responsibility," Danny put in. "I should have seen you personally before I took Hal with me."

Big Ed scowled. "I'll take care of you later." He turned his attention to his cowering son. "Now get on home where you belong!"

He cuffed Hal on the side of the head with his hand. "And be quick about it!"

Danny started to speak, impulsively, but Kay put a restraining hand on his arm.

Big Ed turned back to Danny. "You haven't heard the last of this yet, Orlis! I'm warning you! Nobody messes with Big Ed Seybold and gets away with it!"

With that he shoved Hal up the narrow path ahead of him and strode angrily away.

Danny stared after him.

"Poor Hal," Kay murmured.

"I hope Big Ed isn't too hard on him," Danny said. "I actually feel responsible."

There was a short silence.

"But I'm not sorry Hal went along with me," Danny went on. "God used it to challenge Hal to become a Christian."

Kay's face lighted. "How wonderful!"

She slipped her hand through the crook in his arm. "That makes our having to stay home from the mission field worthwhile."

Danny looked down at her tenderly. "You can say that again."

Together they walked up the narrow path toward their little home.

THE DANNY ORLIS SERIES

The Danny Orlis series, by Bernard Palmer, delivers a blend of adventure, mystery, and suspense through various settings—from the Canadian wilderness to Guatemalan jungles. Danny Orlis, an adept outdoorsman, skilled athlete, and committed Christian, employs his quick thinking, calm bravery, and biblical solutions to confront everyday problems and hair-raising dangers. Early stories focus on Danny navigating school life, sports, and outdoor challenges, while in later books, Danny and his wife Kay provide wisdom and guidance to youngsters facing lifelike situations and challenges. Having sold over two million copies, this series has made Palmer a renowned author in Christian youth literature. Palmer is also the author of the Felicia Cartright series and various other series for Christian youth.

AVAILABLE FROM WWW.ANEKOPRESS.COM

9 798889 360001